More Tales Joe Zone

Nine Entertaining Stories

Joe B. Stallings, Jr.

outskirts
press

More Tales from the Joe Zone
Nine Entertaining Stories
All Rights Reserved.
Copyright © 2023 Joe B. Stallings, Jr.
v2.0

This is a work of fiction. Names, characters, businesses, places, events, locales, and incidents are either the products of the author's imagination or used in a fictitious manner. Any resemblance to actual persons, living or dead, or actual events is purely coincidental.

The opinions expressed in this manuscript are solely the opinions of the author and do not represent the opinions or thoughts of the publisher. The author has represented and warranted full ownership and/or legal right to publish all the materials in this book.

This book may not be reproduced, transmitted, or stored in whole or in part by any means, including graphic, electronic, or mechanical without the express written consent of the publisher except in the case of brief quotations embodied in critical articles and reviews.

Outskirts Press, Inc.
http://www.outskirtspress.com

ISBN: 978-1-9772-5971-4

Cover Photo © 2023 www.gettyimages.com. All rights reserved - used with permission.

Outskirts Press and the "OP" logo are trademarks belonging to Outskirts Press, Inc.

PRINTED IN THE UNITED STATES OF AMERICA

Contents

Introduction		v
1	The Vacation	1
2	I Am a Nice Man—Really, I Am	34
3	Too Much Trouble	57
4	The Letters from the Train	80
5	The Poem and Plagiarism	97
6	You Can't Resign	117
7	You Still Have to Pay for It	133
8	Vacationing on Cornouss	167
9	Braun, Victoria, and the Mob	186

Introduction

I do break a few *rules* of writing.

One, don't use a big word when a simple word will do. I sometimes use archaic words. Why? Because when I read a story, I like to learn new words.

Two, don't leave things unexplained. I don't explain everything, as I think a person's imagination is part of the story.

Three, do not use facts in a fiction story. I like learning new things, so I throw in a fact here and there, but they fit and don't disrupt the story.

Four, yes, I use the word *that* occasionally when it isn't necessary. Sometimes it sounds better to me. Besides, if you diagram the sentence, you diagram *that* in the sentence even if it's not written.

Even though my stories are fiction, several proofreaders have gotten confused in one story because a famous person who is sent a letter is deceased at the time the story takes place. I believe the proofreaders were trying to come up with all kinds of plot twists to explain it—was it a code name for someone, etc. All I can say is it's fiction; pretend the person is still living.

I will define the word *contronym* for you as it is not in many dictionaries. A contronym is a word that can mean opposite things. For example, the archaic word *anon* is a favorite of mine. It can mean any of the following: immediately, soon, occasionally, at another time, or later.

When I use the word *blond*, I spell it without the letter e. *The Chicago Manual of Style* (*CMOS*) doesn't address using the word blond. The *CMOS* editors, however, like the position of *The Associated Press Stylebook*, which is that blond should be spelled without the e unless the word is being quoted.

I've already told you I like to use archaic words, but I can't promise that I have always used them correctly. After all, we know how to use most words correctly because we have heard them spoken correctly, and we almost never hear archaic words. We say, "She is wearing a long yellow dress." We don't say, "She is wearing a yellow long dress." We say it correctly not because we know the grammar rule that an adjective of size comes before an adjective of color, but because we've heard it spoken that way.

In one story I use a word I made up, *trailrod*, which sent proofreaders searching for a word that doesn't exist. Imagine it is what it sounds like, which will be close enough.

I like em-dashes, semicolons, and colons. Sometimes I go light with commas if they disrupt the flow of the sentence, which both introductory adverbs and introductory phrases do now and again. Also, you don't need a comma before a coordinating conjunction if it is connecting two short independent clauses. To me, an independent clause with five or fewer words is short, usually. If a comma is missing, I almost certainly left it out on purpose.

One of my stories has a part that relates to Ukraine and Russia. I wrote the story before the Russian invasion of Ukraine. It is part of what I believe is an entertaining story, and I am certainly not belittling the war and the suffering the Ukrainian people are experiencing—the same with World War II. Two of my stories take place then.

My stories are meant to be entertaining and fun. It was truly enjoyable writing them.

1
The Vacation

Annalease and Kendrick, seventeen-year-old twins, were doing homework at a table in the large reception room of their father's office. The room included a receptionist's desk—forever vacant as a public defender couldn't afford a receptionist— a sofa, a chair, a water cooler, an entire wall of windows, and waist-high shelves crammed with law books. Interspersed on the walls hung grim prints by famous artists, including Vincent van Gogh's *The Potato Eaters*.

Annalease and Kendrick usually stopped by their dad's office on their way home from high school. In addition to getting their homework done, they had opportunities to help their dad with odds and ends and to soak in life experiences without enduring the experiences.

Their dad's clients usually chitchatted while waiting in the reception area and seemed unconcerned about telling the twins the truth. Yet those same clients weren't veridical with the twins' father despite lawyer-client confidentiality. As a result, the twins knew a lot of things that other kids didn't, such as how to break and enter, how to make fake ID cards, how to talk your way out of a traffic ticket, how to bypass low-grade alarm systems, and who was giving the mayor money under the table.

A man who appeared a bit disheveled walked into the office. Mayhap *disheveled* is a bit harsh. After all, he looked no worse than Peter Falk in the TV show *Columbo*.

"May we help you?" Kendrick asked as he stood.

"Yeah, like, I got an appointment at three with Mister . . ." The man pulled a business card out of his pocket and squinted at it. "Jenkins."

"We're waiting for him too. He'll be back in a couple of minutes." Kendrick pulled out a chair at the table where he and Annalease were sitting. If the twins were bonhomie, they noticed the client's nattering would start sooner rather than later.

After a minute the client piped up: "Shame them going after kids these days. What y'all up for?"

"Animal napping," Annalease said. "But we didn't do it."

"Yeah, me neither. Stealing the ring I mean, not the animal napping."

Annalease and Kendrick nodded.

"I mean, I was there. Can't deny that cuz the police found me conked out in back of the pawnshop. But I didn't have the ring, so I couldn't have pinched it. They found my prints on the safe, but only cuz I was 'bout to topple over and put my hand out to stop my fallin'."

Kendrick and Annalease nodded afresh.

"Well, I had been holding the ring earlier cuz Mick gave it to me to look at. It had a large fancy capital E on it. Didn't look like nothin' special. Mick seemed real interested in the paper that was in the box with the ring. Where's my manners; I'm Louie, Louie Selzer of the Chicago Selzers."

"How do you do? I'm Annalease and this is my brother Kendrick."

"Nice to meet you two, I'm sure."

"I told them—the police that found me—that I slipped and hit my head. Not sure what really happened. Felt kinda like I got conked on the head."

"Oh," Annalease said.

Kendrick smiled slightly.

"It was Russell that broke into Trust Me and took the ring out of the safe. I didn't have no idea he was plannin' that. I thought we was just out for a stroll."

"Trust Me?" said Kendrick.

"Yeah, Mick Owens's pawnshop over on Fourth and Berwick."

"This Russell . . . is he a friend of yours?" Annalease asked.

"Russell? Yeah, sure . . . I mean . . . yeah, yeah, he is. Russell Winston is one of my oldest friends. He owns a pawnshop down at Coral Springs, The Easy Dollar. He come up to celebrate my birthday with me—nice guy, only friend who bothered. Even Twiggy, my girl—so I reckoned—didn't show." Louie hung his head.

At that, Mr. Jenkins entered the reception area.

"Ah, Mr. Selzer, please come into my office."

Louie stood, turned to the twins, and said, "Good luck." Then he followed Mr. Jenkins into the office.

"Animal napping?" Kendrick asked Annalease.

"First thing that came to mind. Haven't you seen Mom taking one of Dad's goldfish now and then?"

"No. Why would she do that? Dad loves those goldfish."

"When I inquired, all she said was, 'I'm borrowing them until your dad assents.'"

"Assents . . . to what?"

"I couldn't say. But that reminds me: this morning I did see Mom putting goldfish back into the tank."

"Maybe Dad finally complied."

They both wondered—to what exactly.

"So, Louie—guilty?" asked Annalease.

"I think you would agree we're talking about burglary here, not robbery."

"Yes. It doesn't appear that a weapon or the threat of using a weapon occurred. And it sounds as if he was an accessory and not an accomplice since he wasn't aware of what Russell was planning and went along only after it started. Russell must have knocked Louie out and taken the ring. And the police certainly won't be looking for it at a pawnshop two and a half hours away as it seems that Louie didn't tell the police about Russell."

"Agreed," said Kendrick.

The twins left the matter there—for the moment.

The following day the twins, as usual, were studying at the conference room table in their father's office when a woman walked in. That was unusual—a woman—and the fact that she was both sanguine and svelte made it even more so. She was dressed as you would expect a sanguine and svelte woman to be dressed—fashionably. She wore a large hat on her blond hair, sunglasses, and held a handkerchief in one hand.

"May we help you?" Annalease said as she stood.

"Oh, *oui*," the woman said with a French accent. Holding the handkerchief in front of her mouth, she continued: "You must . . . my, you're more lovely than I imagined; quite sagacious too, I expect. Your father must be very proud. I'm Ms. Kimble, Twinkle Kimble."

Both Annalease and Kendrick excelled at feigning, so

neither showed surprise. Mr. Jenkins appeared at the door at just that moment.

"Ms. Kimble," Mr. Jenkins said, seemingly startled. He glanced at Annalease and Kendrick while his face turned red. He looked back to Ms. Kimble. "I . . . ah . . . wasn't expecting you. Next time, please make an appointment."

Ms. Kimble extended her hand, indicating she expected it to be kissed, but Mr. Jenkins quickly shook it instead.

"*Oui,* certainly, but life is full of surprises. "Your children, they're lovely and—"

"Yes, yes, they are. Please, come into my office."

After the office door closed, Annalease and Kendrick stared at each other trying to suss out the situation.

After a minute Mr. Jenkins popped his head out of his office, and the twins heard Twinkle Kimble utter in her French accent, "It's not immoral to . . ."

"Kids, go on home. I'll be there some . . . er, soon," Mr. Jenkins said before he quickly closed and locked the door.

Kendrick and Annalease knew to refrain from discussing Ms. Kimble. They didn't have enough information to know anything. But one thing they did know—assumptions would take them down the wrong path and lead to trouble. Still, despite knowing better, they aberrated.

"Kendrick, did you get her—"

"Picture? No," replied Kendrick.

"Should we tell Mom?"

"And what exactly would we tell her?"

Annalease shrugged and the twins headed home.

When Charles Jenkins arrived two hours later, the twins were doing homework at the breakfast table.

"Is Mom home yet?" Mr. Jenkins asked.

"Not yet," Kendrick said.

The twins noticed that their father's hair was mussed, and his shirttail was partially hanging out. They gave each other a sideways glance.

"Good," their father said, and he headed upstairs.

"Well?" Annalease said.

"Maybe a gust of wind tussled his hair," Kendrick suggested. "And maybe he fumbled tucking his shirt in."

Annalease frowned.

Kendrick continued: "We would need to give Mom facts, and the only thing we can say is that Dad met with a woman client—not exactly an illicit activity."

"Something can be true," replied Annalease, "even if you can't evince it."

Annalease and Kendrick were doing homework at the conference room table when a clean-shaven man with a fresh haircut and wearing a suit and tie—not typical of their dad's clients—marched into the office.

"May we help you?" Annalease asked.

"Yes, I have an appointment with Mr. Jenkins. I'm Thomas Goodall."

"Have a seat," Annalease said as she pulled out a chair at the conference room table. "Mr. Jenkins will be back shortly."

"Thank you," said Mr. Goodall as he took his seat.

A few minutes passed without Mr. Goodall saying a single word, but the twins had a contingency plan for such cases.

"Mr. Goodall," Kendrick said, "have you spoken to Mr. Jenkins about your case?"

"No, I haven't."

"Then I can go ahead and prepare some notes for his

review. If you'll follow me to the desk, please."

Kendrick seated himself on one side of the desk with Mr. Goodall on the other.

Kendrick opened a drawer and pulled out a yellow legal pad. "You were arrested for what?"

"Animal cruelty."

"When was this?"

"June 15."

"And what were the circumstances?"

"I was walking Sammy, and my neighbor—Miss Goody Two-shoes—complained that the leash was too tight, but Sammy could breathe just fine. The policeman arrested me despite my plea."

"Sammy is a . . . ?"

"A trout."

"A trout? Sammy is a fish?"

"I thought I said that."

"Mr. Goodall, can you explain how you could take your trout for a walk?"

By that point Annalease had propped up her elbows on the table and rested her chin on her fists, her brain enthralled.

"Certainly. Sammy is just shy of a foot long. I scoop him out of the fish tank, put a leash on him, and place him in the portable fishbowl. Then I set the fishbowl in a red wagon and pull the wagon around the neighborhood. He likes to get out and see people and observe life in the neighborhood. He's especially fond of one of Mrs. Pearson's tropical fish—Carmen, I believe.

"Why does he need a leash if he's in a fishbowl?"

"That's the law."

"The law?"

"Yes, if you review the city ordinances, you'll find that any pets taken outside are required to be on a leash. I have been fined before for not having him on a leash."

Kendrick regretted that he had invoked the contingency plan.

Fortunately, Mr. Jenkins arrived just then. "Oh, and what have we here?" he asked.

"Mr. Jenkins, this gentleman, Mr. Goodall, needs your help," Kendrick explained. "He's been charged with animal cruelty."

"Animal cruelty?"

"Yes sir."

"So, Mr. Goodall, have you been walking your trout again?" asked Mr. Jenkins.

Kendrick and Annalease gawked at each other.

"Yes. Yes, I have."

"On a leash I suppose?"

"Yes sir."

"Mr. Goodall, please step into my office and we'll address the matter."

Mr. Jenkins picked up the yellow legal pad, wrote something, handed it back to Kendrick, and followed Mr. Goodall into the office. Annalease peeked over Kendrick's shoulder, and they both read the note:

Call 555-1212 and tell the folks at the psychiatric hospital that Mr. Swinson is out again, and they can pick him up here.

On Saturday morning the twins ate breakfast while watching the local news. A short segment anent an event from 1975—Junko Tabei becoming the first woman to reach the peak of Mount Everest—came on. Ms. Tabei was an inspiration. She made most of her climbing equipment and clothes so she could afford the climb. She almost died when an avalanche buried her, but fortunately some Sherpas rescued Ms. Tabei. After several days of recuperating on the slopes, she continued the ascent.

The following news item concerned a dispute between the communists who cracked the whip in China and a zoo in Coral Springs over a panda that was residing there. The panda was on loan to the zoo, and the communists wanted it back. But US law prevented the return of a living being to a country run by communists, so the communists sued to get the panda back. The court, however, ruled that the panda qualified as a living being.

Annalease and Kendrick glanced at each other and smiled.

"I saw in this morning's paper that Louie Selzer was convicted," Annalease said.

"Yes, a shame too. Ten years in prison—a pretty harsh sentence."

"At most he should have gotten six months, considering."

"Mr. Winston's pawnshop is in Coral Springs, isn't it?"

"That's right. Has Mom told you that Coral Springs is where we're going on vacation in two months? Are you thinking what I'm thinking?"

"Maybe." No matter how Delphic their conversation, one twin could well-nigh tell what the other was thinking within seconds.

"Yes, a call to action I'd say. We could return the ring to the rightful owner and get Louie released in the process. And I'd like to pull the 'thank you for staying with us' prank. I've got *beaucoup* great ideas to spice up the letter."

"Annalease, I think the thank-you-letter prank borders on cruelty."

"As long as it just borders, it's a go."

"We do need to come up with new ventures so we don't get completely bored," Kendrick suggested. "Lying in the sun all day, yuck. What a waste of time. Are you ready for the camping trip next weekend?"

"I will be. Remind me to thank Mom for setting it up," Annalease said with a smirk. "Packing us off on a camping trip with other teenagers isn't my idea of a grand weekend."

"You know Mom. She likes to think she is broadening our horizons with vacations and camping trips."

"Well the vacations certainly do."

They both laughed.

Late that Friday afternoon, after their parents' goodbye hugs, the twins drove to the high school, pulled into the parking lot, and prepared to load their gear onto the bus. The bus would take the group to the Happy Hunted Camp—not exactly the best name for a camp—a two-hour drive to the base of the Ranger Mountains.

Anon before the bus was to leave, Mrs. Arness made an announcement: "Sorry ladies and gentlemen, you need to grab your belongings and go home. A sudden storm wreaked havoc at the camp. Everything was damaged—the cabins, caves, and caldaria."

The students on the bus glanced at their partners with a frown. *Caldaria*. Annalease and Kendrick knew that caldaria—a word not found in most dictionaries—was not exactly the right word to use. After all, the bathhouses were not in ancient Rome.

"I guess you should expect that from a Latin teacher," said Annalease.

"Forsooth," replied Kendrick with a grin.

The twins decided to take in a movie instead of going directly home. It was classical movie night at the downtown theater, and *Rendezvous* was showing, one of their favorites. After the movie they headed home.

"Let's wait until tomorrow to unload," Kendrick said.

"Sounds fine," Annalease said. "Don't want to wake up Mom and Dad. You think we should have called them about the camping trip being canceled?"

"Naw. They'll realize it in the morning when they see the car."

"Okay."

They were tiptoeing down the hallway when their parents' bedroom door—which was at the end of the hallway and faced them—opened. Their father emerged wearing his robe. He stared at the floor as he walked.

"Ah, Twinkle, you're utterly satiating ... unlike my wife."

"*Oui.*"

The twins stopped dead in their tracks, eyes wide.

By then their dad was only a few feet from them. He looked up and said, "Oh, my God!"

"Dad, you have to stop this," Annalease whispered. "And you have to tell Mom."

Mr. Jenkins turned toward his bedroom and loudly said, "Ms. Kimble, my children are home. They want us to stop. And they want me to tell my wife about you."

At that moment Ms. Kimble, wearing a negligee, appeared in the bedroom doorway, and glanced down the hall; the light was very dim.

Ms. Kimble smiled, curtsied, and meekly said, "*Oui.*" Then she pulled off the blond wig and in their mother's voice, said, "Consider it done. Annalease and Kendrick, y'all sleep on the sofas tonight and turn on some music; I'm not done with your father yet."

Mr. Jenkins looked overheated with half his blood loitering about his face.

"Dad," Kendrick said, chuckling, "you need to calm down. You're going to need the blood elsewhere."

Annalease poked Kendrick hard in the ribs and pulled him toward the stairs. "Not another word."

The twins didn't sleep well. Perhaps the sofas weren't comfortable.

The following Friday, the twins were at their dad's office. The embarrassment from the previous weekend had dissipated—mostly. In walked a gentleman dressed as if he were going to church but sans a jacket.

"Excuse me. I'm here to see Mr. Jenkins."

"He'll be back shortly," replied Kendrick, and he pulled out a chair at the conference room table.

The man sat. After a few minutes the man pulled out his wallet and placed bills on the table to press out the wrinkles.

"You play?" asked Annalease.

"Play?"

"Monopoly," Annalease said. "I see you have Monopoly money."

"Nah, this is real money."

Kendrick and Annalease both wondered if they still had the number to the psychiatric hospital.

"That's why I'm here—money laundering. But the assistant district attorney told Mick, my boss, that the charges would be dropped since they couldn't make a case."

"I don't follow," said Annalease.

"Well," the man said as he peeked over his shoulder and then back at the twins, "it was my idea, and it's working swell. At first the gang, all of us gangs, started asking local businesses to pay us for protection—I mean, *insurance*—with cryptocurrency because the government can't prove anything. But I discovered that a graph of the rise in the value of cryptocurrency matches exactly a graph of the rise of tulip bulb prices during the 1637 tulip craze. Even Sir Isaac Newton went broke investing in tulips in those days. Tulips are one of my hobbies.

"Anways, when a business wants to pay us in crypto now, we say no. It's not a legitimate tool for commerce because its value bounces all over kingdom come. You can't make plans if you don't know what it will be worth next week, next month, or next year—or even tomorrow. You have to convince other people it's worth something, and you can't unless they're suckers. Yeah, I know, there are always a few rich suckers. Well, maybe more than a few. Anyhow, that's what spurred me to use Monopoly money."

"I see," said Kendrick. "So how does it work?"

"Well, we bought up one thousand Monopoly games and gave all the play money serial numbers . . . well, not exactly serial numbers . . . the numbers are random. They include letters too. We keep a list of all the serial numbers so no one can buy a game and write numbers on the money to use it. We call the bills *mop*. We encouraged the business to let us use mop in their establishments to purchase things. And they can use mop to pay us for their insurance. If they don't have enough mop to pay, we'll still take cash. It's a form of barter, after a fashion, and it works like a dream. And it keeps the police off our patios."

Mr. Jenkins appeared in the reception area and said, "Mr.

Climbow, you can leave. All the charges have been dropped."

"Thanks," Mr. Climbow said, and he stood to leave. But as he did, he gave each twin a mop bill and a wink. "Treat yourselves at any of the shops on Twelfth Avenue."

The twins were in their dad's office conversing with Fire-crack Jack, the alleged safecracker. The twins arranged the meeting when they knew their dad would be in court.

"So," said Fire-crack Jack, "you want me to case this place and give you the lowdown?"

"That's right," said Annalease.

"You want me to go ahead and—"

"No, no. I'll need a few lessons from you. Kendrick and I will handle it."

Fire-crack Jack shrugged. "So be it."

"Do you mind helping us with this?" Kendrick asked.

"Nah. I owe you one for getting me off the hook for that Wells Fargo job that Bennie the Beedle did."

Their vacation would start in a month, but on this day Annalease and Kendrick were in their dad's office since they studied most of the time, even in the summer. Their father wasn't in but was on his way.

A young man entered the office. He was twenty-five or so and was wearing jeans and a T-shirt.

"Mr. Jenkins in?" he asked.

"Not yet," said Kendrick, "but he'll be here shortly."

"Thanks. I'm Vard Andrews. I'm out on bail for theft."

"Oh, and what did you steal?" asked Annalease.

Vard was nonchalant about the matter, and Annalease was a bit too foursquare on occasion—well, always really.

"They say I stole a bridge."

"Wow, the bridge on Highway 124 where it crosses the Apalachee River?" asked Annalease.

"That's the one."

Kendrick laughed while shaking his head. "That's a new one on me. Good thing that's not a main road. I didn't realize the bridge was missing."

"Metal bridge, not too big, but it took us all night."

"Us?"

"Yeah, me, my sister, and some of her gal pals from her auto shop class at Capone High."

The school was named for Beauregard Capone, the county's most famous alum, not for the other guy.

"Fortunately, the highway curves into the bridge on both sides. We put up plenty of Bridge-Closed signs and flashing lights. A week or so before the job, we went fishing off the bridge several times to take measurements, figure out what tools we needed, spray plenty of WD-40, and the like. We rented a small crane truck to help lift some of the pieces and a flatbed rig to haul everything away. We worked all night, but we got 'er done."

"Where's the bridge now?" Kendrick asked.

"Don't know. I stopped at the Jiffy Mart at the intersection of highways 124 and 326 to use the bathroom, and somebody stole the truck. I shouldn't have left the motor running. Had to report the truck stolen; I sure couldn't afford to pay for it. I could always say the bridge wasn't on it when I had it. Don't know how they tagged me with the theft. I'm certainly not going to fess up. I could lose my job at the junkyard and get my sister into trouble. Besides, it'd embarrass my dad more than it already has."

"Who's your dad?" Annalease asked.

"Judge Andrews, the superior court judge."

Annalease and Kendrick stared at each other. They knew the judge somewhat.

Mr. Jenkins walked in. "Ah, Mr. Andrews," said Mr. Jenkins, "please come into my office."

"Yes, sir. You need to know, sir, I'm innocent. I know nothing about this theft. I mean a bridge . . . my gosh."

"Of course. Come along."

After the door to Mr. Jenkins's office closed, Kendrick said, "Holy cow, are we in a spot now."

Annalease's eyes widened as she shrugged. *Not really*, she thought.

It was only a week before their vacation, and the twins were in their dad's office. "Oh, by the way," Annalease said, "Mom and Dad have agreed to detour through New York City on our way to Coral Springs next week."

"Uh-oh," said Kendrick. "Do I want to know about this?"

"I reminded Mom and Dad that we studied the history of New York City this past year, and we wanted to spend a few hours milling about Wall Street. I didn't tell them we were going to visit the icon of St. Nicholas the Wet at the Holy Trinity Ukrainian Church in Brooklyn. They're going to drop us off on Wall Street while they do their thing, and we'll take a cab to the church."

"Why?" Kendrick asked with a fearful expression.

Annalease pulled a couple of items from her book bag,

gave them to Kendrick, and said, "Read these two articles."

"What are they?"

"One's an article from a 1954 Ukrainian newsletter. The other is from a 1967 Ukrainian American periodical."

Kendrick read both articles—twice—and then said, "Annalease, any plot you have regarding this would be tortuous beyond belief. Surely it doesn't involve taking the icon of St. Nicholas the Wet or, heaven forbid, looking for the body of—"

"Not the body of . . . but the bones of. They should be in a small to medium-sized box, not a casket. Ukraine wants Prince Yaroslav's bones back. After all, he's been missing from St. Sophia in Kyiv since WWII. The Ukrainians just discovered that his bones were missing last year when they opened the box. As you can tell from these articles, the bones are in Brooklyn. We can get them. I'm sure of it."

"You think so, do you?"

"Yes, because of this." Annalease pulled a box out of her backpack, set it in front of Kendrick, and opened it.

"Oh . . . my . . . gosh! That's not the missing one made in 1909 for—"

"Yes, commissioned by Czar Nicholas II for his mother, the wife of Czar Alexander III: the missing Fabergé Alexander III commemorative egg."

"Annalease, that's worth millions, maybe tens of millions of dollars. How on earth did you get it?"

"From Kristonovia Jackson. She's a member of the Ukrainian CIA, so to speak. The egg is a hot potato for the Ukrainians. They can't let the Russians find out they have it because Russia considers any missing Fabergé eggs theirs. And the Ukrainians are more than happy to trade it for the bones of Prince Yaroslav, as Ukraine considers itself the political heir of the Kievan Rus federation. Having his bones back in Kyiv would be a tremendous symbolic victory."

"How does having the egg help us get the bones?" Kendrick asked.

"Ah, so you're *in*."

"It was only a question."

The corners of Annalease's mouth arced into a knowing smile. "Well, to answer your question, one of the members of the church's board is a Fabergé egg connoisseur. He used to go to Malcolm Forbes's parties to study his collection of Fabergé eggs. He's willing to unlock the vault and look the other way while we replace the box of bones with the box containing the Alexander III commemorative."

Kendrick's head was spinning. He was thinking of their established plans: the counterfeit US dollars, getting the ring back to the rightful owner while getting Louie out of jail, and, of course, the letter gag. That was more than enough excitement for one vacation. But from an early age, Kendrick knew Annalease had plenty of gumption and that he'd have a better chance toppling the Eiffel Tower with a wrench and a Q-tip than persuading Annalease to change her mind about *any* plans.

"Speaking of vacation plans, here are the letters I typed," said Annalease. "One will go in the box with the ring, and the other we'll send to Mrs. Jackson Minnow."

"I know I agreed to the letters earlier, but since then I have discovered that the government can track down anyone who writes a Word document by the microcode in the letters when they're printed."

"I read the same thing. That's why I typed them on Dad's old typewriter, a Remington Super-Riter typewriter that he used as an Associated Press reporter in Moscow. I'm confident the government doesn't have a copy of all the type from every typewriter ever made, much less a list of who owns which typewriter."

Annalease and Kendrick were each reading a book in the van's back seat on the way to Coral Springs via Brooklyn. When they reached Coral Springs, they would be staying in a hotel across from their parents. For the past three years Mr. and Mrs. Jenkins had treated their vacations with the kids as separate events. They wanted the twins to be on their own as long as they stayed together. They should be able to do the things they wanted to without any encumbrances from their parents, which would help them learn to be independent adults. They also were given five hundred dollars each for spending money.

The twins already had or knew the following:
- The letter to Mrs. Jackson Minnow, wife of the Coral Springs mayor.
- Lots of information on the city zoo. They would be starting their jobs there on Monday. They would work only one day. They had called the zoo several days before to ensure the dozen freestanding, full-length mirrors that they had sent to the zoo had arrived. They were in the storeroom.
- Two blow-up punching bags.
- A bear costume and a lion costume.
- A box of disposable latex gloves.
- The room number where they were staying. It was one floor above the room the FBI had under surveillance. It was a precaution in case they needed an alibi.

- An oscillating fan.
- Information on The Easy Dollar, Russell Winston's pawnshop.
- And, of course, the Fabergé Alexander III commemorative egg.

"Oh, Annalease, I forgot to tell you," Mrs. Jenkins said, "someone called yesterday, and he asked me to give you a message."

"What's the message?"

"'The honey from the panda is ready to be collected as arranged.' What does that mean?"

Kendrick glanced at Annalease with raised eyebrows, wondering what she would say.

"Kendrick and I will be visiting the zoo and bought some honey to feed the panda," Annalease replied.

Kendrick smiled at that.

"Oh," Mrs. Jenkins said. "How nice."

Kendrick thought, *If you only knew.*

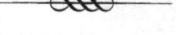

Brooklyn

The Jenkins's car pulled up to the curb on Wall Street.

"Here you go, kids," Mrs. Jenkins said. "Your dad and I are going to tour the Brooklyn Museum. Call us when you're ready to be picked up."

"Okay," Kendrick replied as Annalease followed him out of the car. She was wearing the backpack with the egg inside. Their parents drove off, and the twins headed down the street to catch a cab. It dropped them at the front door of the Holy Trinity Ukrainian Church in Brooklyn.

"Why didn't you tell Mom and Dad to pick us up at the New York City Public Library?" Kendrick asked. "Isn't that where we hand the bones to Kristonovia Jackson?"

"Yes, it is, but I'm avoiding telling anyone anything until it's necessary. We need to go into the church and sit in a certain pew on the far right for one minute. I sit in the fifth row from the back. You take the sixth row just in front of me. And don't act like you know me. After the minute has elapsed, we'll go to the hallway on the right side of the church and walk to the fifth door on the left."

They entered and took their respective seats. Kendrick heard shuffling and creaking sounds behind him.

"What are you doing?" Kendrick asked Annalease without turning around.

"Just adjusting the kneeler; it's broken."

Funny, he thought: *my pew doesn't have kneelers; budget cuts, no doubt.* A minute later they both stood up and approached the altar before veering into the hallway. Their footsteps echoed on the marble floor as they marched in unison. When they reached the fifth door on the left, Annalease knocked a couple of times, and they both entered.

No one was there. The room was sparse but well-lit. In the middle of the room was a long table large enough to seat eight on each side and one on each end. Annalease and Kendrick took in their surroundings as they moved to the table's far side. Annalease took off her backpack, set it on the floor, took out the box with the egg, and placed it on the table in front of her.

"Are we early?" Kendrick asked.

"A couple of minutes. You remember what Mr. Rader looks like?"

"Of course. You only showed me his picture a zillion times."

A few minutes later a woman entered. *A woman?*

"Ah, you're here, very good," she said.

"Who are you?" Annalease asked.

"Lisa. Mr. Rader was taken ill last night and has given me all the information. We can proceed with the arrangement. I assume the egg is in the box. Will you open it, please?"

Kendrick was growing nervous. *Who is this woman?* He started shaking a bit; but Annalease never missed a beat.

"Certainly, but where are the bones?"

Lisa walked over to an interior door, unlocked it, opened it, stepped inside, and turned on the light. On a small table sat a box. Lisa brought the box over and set it on the table near the egg.

"Here are the bones," Lisa said.

Annalease sat at the table, opened the box with the egg, and pushed it over to Lisa to examine.

Lisa pulled out a magnifying glass and spent a minute examining the egg. Then she pushed the egg back to Annalease and stood.

Annalease closed the box.

"Yes, this will do," Lisa said. Then in a boisterous voice she announced, "The egg is genuine."

At those words, two masked figures burst into the room with machine guns at the ready.

"Oh, dear me," Lisa said. "It's a stickup."

No one else spoke or moved. Even the thieves appeared taken aback, thunderstruck that they were armed with machine guns to rob two teenagers perhaps. After an awkward fifteen seconds, Lisa finally piped up. "What do you want—the box with the egg?"

The thieves glanced at each other, turned back to Lisa, and nodded.

"I guess you should take the box and put it in the thieves' bag," Lisa said, looking at Kendrick. The smaller of the two thieves pulled a bag from his jacket pocket.

Kendrick reached down to pick up the box. With his hand shaking so, he knocked the box off the table and onto the backpack sitting on the floor.

"For goodness' sake," Annalease said as she picked up the box, carried it to the thieves, and dropped it into the bag. Then she resumed her position at the table next to Kendrick.

The thieves backed out of the room and closed the door. The echo of footsteps diminished as the thieves sprinted down the hall.

"Well," Lisa said, "Terrible, terrible, but the deal's off." She picked up the box of bones, took it into the small room, and placed it on the table. She then backed out of the room and locked its door. "I'm sure you can find your way out," Lisa said as she left, leaving the door open for the twins.

How considerate of her thought Annalease.

As the twins were trudging down the hall, Kendrick was still shaking, trying to sort out the ramifications of what had just happened. As they made their way through the church, Annalease stopped at the fifth pew from the back and sat exactly where she had been sitting a few minutes prior.

"Come, sit with me," Annalease said to Kendrick.

"I don't think praying will help us now."

After Kendrick was seated, Annalease reached under the pew in front of her and pulled out a box three feet long and one foot wide.

"What's that?" Kendrick asked.

"The bones of Prince Yaroslav, of course. And this," she said as she pulled a box out of her backpack, "is the egg, which I'll leave in its place. Exchange complete."

"But . . . the egg. I saw you give it to them."

"No, you saw me give them a box with a rock in it. A box that is glued shut. It will take them time to open it since they'll have to be careful not to break the egg they think is inside. It could take hours."

"But . . . the bones. What about them?"

"The box Lisa showed us didn't have any bones in it. Or at least not the bones of Prince Yaroslav. I confirmed that these are his bones when we sat in the pew earlier."

Thirty minutes later they were sitting on the New York City Public Library steps waiting for Kristonovia Jackson while Annalease explained the rest of the story to Kendrick.

"Mr. Rader and I spoke a week ago. He called me on a burner phone as he believed the SVR, the Russian Foreign Intelligence Service, was following him and had tapped his phone. He was concerned the SVR had learned of the egg, so we added fail-safes to the exchange. Sorry I didn't tell you, but your being nervous helped. When you knocked the box off the table, I exchanged it for the other box in my backpack."

"I hope Mr. Rader is okay."

"He's fine. He passed us as we were leaving the church. He was dressed as an Orthodox priest. Remember the priest with the long beard?"

"If you say so."

Just then a woman sat on the steps next to Annalease. Kendrick stood and stepped away a few feet.

"A pretty day, isn't it?" Annalease said.

"Yes. I guess it's a lovely day in Kyiv too," the woman said. "I can feel it in my bones."

"A quote from Chekhov?" Annalease replied.

"No, a quote from Kristonovia," Ms. Jackson said as she winked at Annalease, the coded acknowledgment complete.

"You could have told me," Annalease said.

"Not my place," Kristonovia replied.

Kristonovia Jackson then stood, picked up the box, and proceeded to a twister orange GT500 Mustang waiting at the curb.

Annalease stood, walked over to Kendrick, and said, "Now we can call Mom and Dad."

An hour later the family was back on its way to Coral Springs. It was quiet the rest of the way.

Annalease and Kendrick were in their hotel suite and had finished unpacking. Their parents had gone on to their hotel. Annalease was relaxing on the bed, eyes closed, while Kendrick was unsuccessfully trying to read.

"The government agents we're giving the counterfeit money to, should we tell them about the Easy Dollar?" Kendrick asked.

"No, absolutely not."

"We're really quite a pair, aren't we?"

Annalease smiled without further comment.

"So the FBI agents watching the room below us don't know what we're up to?" Kendrick asked.

"That's right. The CIA knows, but only about the panda."

The next morning at seven, the twins were at the zoo's orientation for new employees. They each had their animal costume in a shopping bag. An hour later the HR manager was finishing up.

"And finally, I shouldn't need to say this since we deal with the public, but I will. No vulgar displays, no cutting-up nonsense, no bad language; treat everyone with respect—and no chewing gum. Today is a free day. Wander around and become familiar with the layout. Tomorrow morning you will get your assignments. Your lockers are in the room next door. I'll hand out your keys. Then you can lock up any personal items and start wandering. And for those of you already wearing your zoo T-shirt identifying you as a zoo employee, good job."

Annalease and Kendrick smiled at each other.

"Now off with you."

After the twins put their animal costumes in their lockers, they headed to the motor pool.

"Excuse me," Kendrick said to a guy in the garage, "we need one of the small utility trucks to take some supplies from storage to the panda room."

"Uh, yeah. Take that one on the end. It's gassed up and the key's in it."

The panda room didn't actually have pandas in it. It was the building you went through to access the panda enclosure.

The twins drove to the storage warehouse, aisle fourteen, storage bin H. There they found fourteen full-length mirrors already assembled. The twins folded the mirrors' legs, loaded seven on the truck, and tied them down. They'd need to make two trips. Between trips they visited their lockers and collected the lion and bear outfits that they would need shortly.

After they unloaded the mirrors from the second trip, they gave the panda room attendant a letter on zoo letterhead. It said the room was to be temporarily closed while Annalease and Kendrick updated a few things.

"Okay," the attendant said. "I'll put the Temporarily Closed sign up, and you can lock the door behind me."

As soon as the attendant left, the twins went to work. Kendrick opened the door that led to the young panda's quarters. The young panda always took a nap between ten thirty and eleven thirty in the morning behind the enclosure's bars so visitors could watch him sleep. Kendrick used his measuring tape to mark spots on the sidewalk between the panda room and the panda's sleeping area. Several months earlier, he had calculated where each mirror needed to be placed. He had double-checked his calculations, and Annalease had rechecked them. It was ten thirty, all the mirrors were in place, and the panda was asleep. The view was perfect. Kendrick wiggled into the bear costume, and Annalease slipped into the lion costume. Then they took up positions by the door and waited.

A few minutes before eleven there were two knocks on the door, a pause, and three more knocks. Kendrick opened the door. The two communist men, one with a briefcase and the other with a large animal carrier, entered the room. They were dressed in casual clothes. Kendrick led them to a table where they could see the panda if they looked left through the door.

"Put the case on the table, please," Kendrick said. "We want to see the fifty thousand."

The man with the briefcase set it down and opened it.

Kendrick reached down, flipped through several bundles of bills, and ensured it was all there.

"Okay," Kendrick said.

"The panda?" the other communist said.

Kendrick pointed to the open door. The mirrors had been arranged so they could see the panda sleeping on the large rock, but the bars were concealed. It appeared as if you could simply walk over and take the panda.

The communist nodded.

Kendrick closed the case, and he and Annalease started for the door while the communists headed for the panda they had just purchased. Once the twins were outside, they raced to the utility truck and sped off. Early on a Monday, the zoo's parking lot was mostly empty. The twins zoomed into the parking lot. A black helicopter belonging to the CIA making noise only slightly above a whisper, the newest high-tech model, swooped into the parking lot and hovered a few feet off the ground. Annalease drove the utility truck by the helicopter without stopping, and Kendrick threw the briefcase into the chopper's open door. Annalease turned right, out of the parking lot exit, then fifty feet farther, turned right again into a Jiffy Mart. She wheeled the utility truck behind the Jiffy Mart, skidding to a stop in front of the dumpster. They couldn't have known a police officer, casually smoking while leaning against his police car, would be there to greet them.

"Okay, you two, out. What exactly are y'all up to?"

They both stepped out of the utility truck. Kendrick started to take the bear's head off when Annalease stopped him and said, "Officer, I'm going to take an identification card out of my lion's suit. I'll do it very slowly; it will explain everything."

The officer unsnapped his gun holster and gripped the handle of his weapon but left it holstered.

"This should be interesting. Let's see what kind of identification card a lion has."

Annalease slowly pulled out the card, turned it so the officer could read it, and held it up to his face.

"Well, dang. Don't that beat all—a bear and a lion."

"Officer, if you would please turn around, the bear and I need to toss these disguises into the dumpster."

"Sure thing," the officer said as he turned, put his hands over his eyes, and started counting to one hundred. "One Mississippi, two Mississippi . . ."

The twins threw their outfits into the dumpster before strolling to the front of the Jiffy Mart where they slipped into a cab they had waiting.

"Already got twenty on the meter," the cabbie said.

Kendrick pulled out a hundred, gave it to the cabbie, and told him which hotel they were staying at. "And keep the change."

"Thanks, bud."

"Can I see it again?" Kendrick asked Annalease.

Annalease pulled the identification card out of her pocket and gave it to Kendrick.

He thought it was so cool. Only one word and two numbers appeared:

Alice
57

The CIA told the local police that an operation involving national security was taking place—which was true—and that anyone with that identification was not to be interfered with, period. It was an operation to collect counterfeit US dollars from the communists who were oppressing the Chinese people. The US government needed some of the fake dollars to examine to find their minuscule flaws.

Back at the hotel, the twins took a well-earned nap: one adventure down, two to go.

The next day the twins mostly relaxed before preparing for that evening's activities. They partially inflated the punching bags, laid out the latex gloves, and moved two lamps to better spots. Then they put the letter, assorted tools, the box to mail the ring, and a stethoscope into the shopping bag.

At one in the morning, they finished inflating the punching

bags, turned on the lamps and the oscillating fan, opened the curtains (but not the sheers), and opened the sliding glass door to the balcony. With the fan oscillating, the punching bags gave the illusion of two people moving to-and-fro. The FBI agents watching the room below theirs would see shadows in their room, thus giving the twins an alibi if needed. Then the twins, carrying the shopping bag with all the items they would need for the night's activities, headed out to hail a cab.

The cabbie dropped them off at an all-night theater that showed movies from the 1930s. They bought tickets and pretended to go inside. Since they had seen *Rendezvous* many times, they could prove they had attended the movie, and it just so happened that the theater was only a block from the Easy Dollar.

Since Fire-crack Jack had scoped out the Easy Dollar for the twins, they were ready. He told the twins where the alarm wires were and which ones to cut without triggering the alarm. Fortunately, Russell had an antique safe that could be opened by listening to the tumblers. Fire-crack had let Annalease practice on some of his models. The twins moved into the alley and crept to the back of the pawnshop where they found the alarm wire and cut it before picking the lock. Once inside, they headed for the safe and Annalease pulled out the stethoscope. After a minute she had the safe opened. It took less than a minute to find the box with the ring and the letter. A fancy E was carved on the face, and the ring was scratched up.

"Okay," said Annalease, "let's put it in our box and drop it off at the post office."

"Yep," Kendrick said. Then he read the letter before putting it into the box with the ring.

Elvis Presley
Memphis, TN

Dear Elvis,

Enclosed is your high-school class ring that was missing. Louie Selzer is serving a ten-year sentence for taking it. But as you can see, he couldn't have taken it as you have it. Also enclosed is the letter of authenticity. We ask that you contact the state's attorney general who believes you rank just below God and have Mr. Selzer released.

All the best,
The Twins of Justice

On the way back to the nearest taxi stand in front of the city's train depot, Annalease and Kendrick passed a post office and mailed the ring. Then they grabbed a cab back to the hotel where they slept soundly.

Although there were several vacation days left, the twins only had one clandestine project remaining, and it was simple enough—mail a letter. Kendrick had agreed to the letter only because the mayor's bribery conviction had been overturned on a technicality, and he was still in office. The letter wasn't to the mayor but to his wife. It was well-known that she ruled the roost, and the twins deemed it the best way to punish the mayor. Kendrick read the letter one more time before sliding it into the envelope.

July 30, 2018
Mrs. Jackson Minnow
135 Main Street
Coral Springs, Florida 12378

Dear Mrs. Minnow,

We want to thank you and your husband, Jackson Minnow, for staying with us at the Moonlight Motel earlier this month. We value all our customers highly and are very sorry for the problem you had. We regret very much that the vending machine in the lobby that dispenses condoms was both broken and out of condoms. We can certainly understand the frustration on Mr. Minnow's part—and yours too, of course. And to compliment you, you look a lot better in person than in the photographs we see in the newspaper now and again. We didn't realize, however, that your hair is blond. If your future stay with us is the same length, only a couple of hours, we'll gladly give you a 50 percent discount on the standard daily rate.

Again, our apologies, and all the best.

Management, the Moonlight Motel

The day after the twins returned home from their vacation, their parents dropped them off and headed to the Catskills on their own, which was a surprise. The twins were scheduled to meet someone at a picnic table in the city park at eleven that morning.

When the twins arrived at their assigned picnic table, no one else was around. But in a jiffy, a man in shorts and a T-shirt approached their table and said, "I wonder how Alice fifty-seven is doing?"

"Hi, Mr. Boulevardier," Annalease replied, using their CIA handler's code name.

"Hello, Annalease, Kendrick. You did a great job with the panda. We discovered a flaw in the counterfeit money, so we'll be able to spot the fakes easily from now on. Funny that you failed to mention your plan to help the Ukrainians. Seems that turned out all right . . . mostly, thank goodness. But I'm afraid we're not going to be able to use you in the future."

"What?" Kendrick said. "We don't tell you about one little thing we planned, and you drop us. That's gratitude."

"We have to. You've been compromised because of your interaction with the communists."

"What do you mean we're compromised?" Kendrick protested. "We were dressed as animals. The communists never saw our faces."

Boulevardier looked at Annalease and said, "He doesn't know?"

Annalease shook her head. "No. He's not as observant as I am."

"Those communists aren't the problem. It's the two thieves who tried to steal the egg. They're SVR agents."

"So they were Russian agents," Kendrick said. "Surely we can work against communists in other countries."

"You don't understand. The SVR agents are your parents."

The End

2
I Am a Nice Man—
Really, I Am

"You only hired three more workers?" Elsa asked her husband Saturday night.

"With three months until Christmas, we need more workers, but I couldn't hire them all," Walter replied.

"Six applied for jobs?" Elsa asked.

Walter's hands stopped crafting the toy on the workbench, and he looked at Elsa with a sad but determined face. They were in what looked like a large barn behind their home in the forest just outside a village in Southern Germany. The barn was a workshop where ten workers, Walter and Elsa's employees, crafted children's toys during the week.

"Yes . . . six. But with the war and the shortages we have, toy sales will be down. I could only hire three."

"The other three, they're Jewish too? Like the rest of our workers?"

"Yes. Tomorrow before we go to Mass, I'll drive them close to the border and give them instructions. With no border fence and no patrols scheduled for the morning, they'll make it to Schaffhausen. I've always thought it amusing that the city of Schaffhausen is part of Switzerland when it's surrounded on three sides by Germany."

"You're not taking them across the border in the truck?" Elsa asked with an inquisitive look.

"No. I can't risk it for only three people," Walter said, shaking his head. "They're all young—they'll make it on their own before dark."

"All this business is such a terrible thing. I'm glad no one's after us, taking our things," Elsa said. "But I wish this was all over—the war, the Nazis. We're doing the right thing, I know, but sometimes I wonder . . . should two old folks like us take this risk? Is it worth it, Walter, doing this?"

Walter paused for a moment before replying. "When the war is over, many Jews will be glad we did. But what we're doing is only a small thing, really, considering what else is happening. I honestly have misgivings and think we're not doing enough. Thankfully, authoritarian governments can never keep all their citizens in line, which gives us the opportunity. We'll be okay."

"What worries me the most is you flashing your law enforcement badge—what is it called, oh yes, your warrant disc—every time you're in Cologne. I can't help thinking that one day your—*our*—luck will run out since you're so keen on flashing it when you really don't need to; and trying to find out more information about that secret German encryption machine, Enigma, that the Nazis use to send coded messages. Goodness me."

"I only flash it sometimes when I'm in Cologne. And can I help it if I want to put the warrant disc to good use. With so many toy buyers headquartered there, my trips don't raise suspicions; and Cologne is a good collection point for the *contraband*. Living so far away, we're not likely to run into anyone who will cause us problems."

Elsa kissed Walter's head and left him alone in the workshop.

Walter wondered if he should stop telling her about all of his extracurricular activities.

Two months earlier—August 1942

"Ugh, you're wearing that. Can't you just take it in your suitcase?" Elsa asked.

"Lounge suit, shirt, tie, broad-brimmed hat, and leather trench coat—what could be better for a trip to Cologne?" Walter replied.

"Perhaps something that doesn't scream 'I'm Gestapo,' you football."

Walter was impressed that Elsa knew the slang for Gestapo.

She continued, "If you're wearing the Luger, I'm not going to hug you goodbye."

"Goody—it's in the suitcase."

On Walter's first night in Cologne, where he would be all week, he was walking downtown deciding what to do when he noticed the theater across the street. It was showing *The Thin Man*—certainly more appealing than the war movie at the theater behind him. As he was about to cross the street, he heard a man's raised voice. Walter turned and saw the man with a woman; he held her tightly by the wrist, then slapped her. Anon, the man's fist was on the way to the woman's face again when it was stopped by Walter's palm. Crafting toys all day makes for strong hands.

"Hey, mister," the man said, "this is none of your business. I'm the police. Let go, or else." The man's arm relaxed as he was in a hurry to pull out his warrant disc, so Walter let go. It was a *copper-colored* warrant disc. "See," he said, "local police." It had the number 622 on it.

"Yes, I see," Walter said as he unbuckled the belt on his trench coat making sure the man saw the Luger in his shoulder holster. The man's face showed uncertainty. Walter slowly pulled out his *silver-colored* warrant disc, his finger hiding the number stamped under the words *Geheime Staatpolizei*, which meant Secret State Police—in other words, Gestapo.

The man's eyes went wide. Walter moved his finger so the man could see the number: Five.

"I'm sorry, Herr . . . "

"Last. Walter Last."

"My wife and I—it's just a small misunderstanding. Everything is fine. Tell him, Clara."

Before Clara could say a thing—if she were going to—Walter inquired, "Your name?"

"Yes, yes, of course, I'm Bruno Zeller."

Walter turned to the woman. "Frau Zeller, where do you live?"

"Here in Cologne."

"Your address please?"

"Is this really—" Herr Zeller began.

Without turning to him, Walter put his hand in front of the man's face to halt him. "Please, go on, Frau Zeller."

Frau Zeller showed a hint of a smile to her rescuer. "One twenty-five Ritter Strasse."

"Fine," Walter said as he pulled out a notebook from his pocket and wrote it down. Walter turned away from the two, took a few steps down the street for dramatic effect, then turned back to the couple.

"I don't live in town, but I'm here often on . . . uh . . . business. Once in a while I'll stop by to say hi and perhaps have a sip of mineral water. I'm not really a beer man. Imagine that—a German who's not a beer man." Walter chuckled to himself, but then his smile faded. "My stopping by could be sooner or later, now or then, spring or fall, night or day, often or never. And I'll want to see Clara's face. It's such a . . . pretty face. The prettiest face I've seen all month, except for my wife's, of course."

Frau Zeller's smile coruscated in the night, while Bruno Zeller appeared like a deer caught in headlights.

"Oh yes—may I recommend the movie across the street? I know it's an American movie, but the main character has a mustache similar to our Leader's. *I'm a nice man—really, I am*." Walter smiled as he turned and walked away.

It was Friday, Walter's last day in Cologne. He was delivering the toys to various buyers. On the way he stopped off at 125 Ritter Strasse. Frau Zeller was slow to answer the door. She had been on the phone with Herr Zeller and saw Herr Last drive up to the house. She was more than happy to mention his arrival to her husband and then answer the door. She invited Walter in and looked to be okay. After his mineral water and a pleasant conversation, Walter told her he'd be on his way. But first he asked her to roll up her sleeves; her arms were not bruised.

When Walter walked around the back of his truck, two men stepped in front of him. A man also stepped behind him. All were Gestapo.

"Herr Last, I am Herr Frank, the Gestapo chief here in Cologne. Your truck keys, please. And let's take a ride to headquarters if you don't mind."

"Of course." The corner of Walter's mouth went up slightly at the thought of another game of cat and mouse.

Thirty minutes later Walter was sitting opposite Herr Frank at his desk. Herr Zeller was on the sofa, and another man was standing by the door. Herr Zeller had passed on information about Walter Last to Herr Frank earlier in the week in an attempt to find out more about him and get some revenge.

Herr Frank began. "Herr Last, I could find no record of a Herr Walter Last in the Gestapo or of your number—five—being used by anyone. If you'd be so kind as to write a confession for impersonating someone in the Gestapo, then we can take you downstairs. If you're accommodating, you'll go to a real prison, not a camp. If I wasn't so curious about you, you'd already be in the basement."

Herr Frank pushed paper and a pen over to Walter for a confession.

Walter smiled and thought, *What luck*. He reached out, took the paper and pen, and started writing. He wrote some numbers and slid the paper back to Herr Frank who looked annoyed after examining it.

"Are you trying to be funny, Herr Last?"

"Not at all. I would strongly advise you to call this number before mistakes are made."

"And whose number would it be?"

"Reichsfuhrer Himmler—Berlin."

The smile deserted Herr Frank's face; his eyes narrowed. He opened a desk drawer, pulled out a telephone ledger, and flipped through it. He stopped, grabbed the number that Walter wrote down, and compared the two.

"I'm afraid, Herr Frank, that I must insist you call the number," Walter said. Walter had seen the number in the telephone ledger—it had the name of Himmler's adjutant Obersturmbannführer Werner Grothmann next to the number. Walter glanced back at Herr Zeller, who was starting to sweat.

Herr Frank dialed the number. "Hello, Obersturmbannführer Grothmann, this is Herr Frank, Gestapo, Cologne."

"Yes, Herr Frank. What is it?"

"We have taken an interest in a man who claims to be in the Gestapo, but there is no record of him or his warrant disc, number five."

"Warrant disc number five, you say?"

"Yes, and this man knows the Reichsfuhrer's number and insisted that we call."

"What's the man's name?"

"Walter Last."

"Describe him to me."

Herr Frank proceeded to describe Walter who had a not-so-subtle grin.

"Please tell me that you haven't harmed this man."

"No, sir, I haven't. He is right here in my office."

"Herr Frank, this man *is* a Gestapo agent. He is not listed because he does special jobs for the Reichsfuhrer. He is not to be harmed or interfered with in any way. Do you understand?"

"Of course."

"Put me on speakerphone," Herr Grothmann requested.

"Walter, I hope you are well, and I am sorry for this mix-up.

It hasn't caused you any inconvenience has it?"

"Werner," Walter replied, "good to speak with you. No, none at all."

"Good."

Walter continued, "Please tell Heinrich I said hello and that I look forward to seeing him later this year. I'll be in Berlin before Christmas delivering some toys to Reich Minister Goebbels."

"I will—and, as always, Himmler sends his best." Herr Grothmann continued, "Herr Frank, I assume that Herr Last is free to go?"

"Yes, of course."

"Good . . . Bye."

Herr Frank looked at Herr Zeller and said, "Herr Zeller, I'll see to it that the local police fire you. Get out."

Zeller left.

Walter stood and said, "Herr Frank, it would be best if Herr Zeller were not fired. I interrupted him hitting his wife the other day, and I don't want him taking his frustrations out on her."

"As you wish."

Walter caught up with Herr Zeller as he was leaving the headquarters.

"Herr Zeller, you will not be fired. Here is my card. Call me if you get fired, and I'll fix it. But not if you hit your wife again. If you do that, you will disappear. Do you understand?"

He nodded gratefully with a timid grin.

At that moment in Berlin, Adjutant Obersturmbannführer Werner Grothmann turned around in his chair. He received calls like this one now and again, although it seemed to be happening more often as of late. He thought back to the day when Himmler's staff was informed about Walter Last. Herr

Last was in his late twenties or early thirties when he dove into a cold river during the winter to save a little boy from drowning. Years later, probably 1937, at Herr Last's request, he was made an honorary Gestapo agent with warrant disc five. After that he was untouchable—Himmler had made that clear. There were even rumors that Herr Last occasionally helped Jews escape to Switzerland and hired them for his toy business. Whenever a report anent Herr Last ended up on Himmler's desk, Reichsfuhrer Himmler returned it with a note that read, "Kindly leave Herr Last alone," words that had saved Walter on more than one occasion.

Walter headed home after leaving Gestapo headquarters. On the way he stopped at a secluded farm nestled deep in the woods. The farm was a bit out of his way, but he had been helping Jews for five years and wasn't going to stop. Since his truck was devoid of toys, he loaded it with Jewish *contraband*, shall we say, and was on his way home. Elsa knew what to do and that Walter would want to take the *contraband* across the border the next morning. She would drive to the border crossing, bring the guards some homemade snacks, and check the duty roster to learn who would be on patrol the next day. Over the past four years, Walter's truck had never been searched crossing the border into Switzerland—something he had skillfully arranged six years earlier.

Six Years Earlier

"So we're in agreement?" Walter asked Elsa.

"Yes. I must say, I never imagined us doing such a thing. How you ever thought of it . . . goodness. You think your being honorary Gestapo will protect us?"

"It should. If Himmler gets a report here or there about me—or us—he will overlook it. It'll help that he's bringing me my own warrant disc with the number five. That should stop most reports concerning us from even going to Berlin."

"Oh, Walter." Elsa sighed. "With all the bad things going on in Germany, I'm glad that our children emigrated to America decades before the First World War. I don't imagine I'd be willing to do this and put their lives at risk if they were still in Germany."

"Himmler will be here soon," Walter warned, "and he said he would bring my silver warrant disc and a couple of outfits for me that the Gestapo normally wears. He'll be all decked out in his SS uniform, and we should get to know him a little better anyway. Then we'll spend part of the day at the two border crossings."

"You've planned this masterfully. Being at the crossings with Himmler during an inspection will ensure that all the border guards and the higher-ups will see you two together."

"I don't know how long we can do this, but we're going to need as much vitamin B as we can get," Walter said.

"Vitamin B?" Elsa asked.

"Friends in high places."

"Ah. If anybody has vitamin B, it's you."

At the border crossing Reichsfuhrer Himmler gave his little speech. "Herr Last is to be given every courtesy when crossing the border. He has carte blanche to cross the border anytime with no hindrance. I have no doubt that even the Führer would be displeased if Herr Last were impeded in conducting his business."

It also helped that Walter always brought some of Elsa's treats; the guards were always in a hurry to attack them.

Border Crossing—Summer 1943

Walter pulled up to the border crossing and got out of his truck. When he first started doing this task, he crossed the border about once a month. Now it was happening six times a month or more. Thanks to what Herr Himmler had said to all the border guards on his visit in 1937, Walter's truck was never searched.

"Herr Last, good to see you again," said Hans, the border guard.

"You too, Hans. More treats for you and the others, as usual."

"You and Frau Elsa—you are just too generous."

"We like to feel we're helping the Fatherland."

"Let me lift the gate for you."

As Walter drove across the border, Hans yelled, "I hope you sell lots of toys."

A few hundred feet down the road, Walter stopped at another gate. The Swiss border guards had never searched his truck either. They knew Walter by then, and he rarely had to show his letter from the Swiss Federal Council instructing them to let his truck pass through the border without inspection. The Council knew what Elsa and Walter were doing and had agreed to cooperate. They had even acquiesced to watch over the *contraband*.

Walter had a bit of a scare now and then. One scare that stood out was when a man in Cologne threatened to expose him. The man, Helmut Kemper, was a purchasing agent for a toy distributor, and Walter was in his office. Walter's truck was full of *contraband,* and he was arranging to bring more toys on a return visit.

"Herr Last, now that our business is finished, I need to take up a personal matter with you."

"Oh, a personal matter?" Walter said, a bit taken aback.

"Yes, the authorities here in Cologne have become . . . how shall I say it? More zealous about Nazi ideology, especially in light of the turn the war has taken."

"You're referring to the surrender of the German Sixth Army at Stalingrad?"

"Yes, and we Jews are being blamed as usual."

"You're Jewish?"

"Yes, but my wife is a gentile, which in the past has protected me. But now they've started rounding up Jewish spouses. I would like for you to meet my wife. She should be arriving any minute."

There was a knock at the door. Herr Kemper walked over and opened it.

In walked a tall blond woman wearing a long black winter coat. Her lips were red, her face pure white, and she had a big smile. The woman addressed Walter.

"Herr Last, I cannot believe it's you. When Helmut told me about you and how you could help us, I knew you were my former high school history teacher."

Walter had taught high school for several years, many years earlier, when the toy business had been slow.

"I'm assuming you're Herr Kemper's wife, but I'm sorry, Frau Kemper, I don't recall . . . wait—you're Clara Fassbender. Of course!"

At that Clara proceeded to give Walter a hug. She had been

one of his better students, and he had high hopes for her future. Herr Kemper sat quietly, allowing them a few minutes to reminisce. Clara was a doctor now, and she and Herr Kemper had two children together.

"Herr Last, do you mind if we get back to the business I was referring to?" asked Herr Kemper.

"Of course—but if you wouldn't mind getting to the point."

"I know all about you and what you are doing. I want you to get me and my family across the border into Switzerland too. As I indicated, I expect to be arrested any day now."

Clara's eyes betrayed a longing look for Walter's help.

Walter sat on the sofa and thought for several minutes. Neither of them interrupted his thoughts.

"I can't. I'm sorry." Walter had to be careful what he said in case it was a trap. "In the past, on occasion, I may have dropped people close to the border and given them instructions regarding what to do if they accidentally found themselves in Switzerland, but I don't do that anymore. The border is mined now and patrolled continuously. And the patrols use dogs."

"Herr Last, I'm sure there are other arrangements you can make. I've made a point to learn a lot about you. It seems there are a few Jews who have information about what you're doing—things that I'm sure you wouldn't want to be known. And if you don't help us, I'll make sure that—"

"Helmut," Clara interrupted, "this is not—"

"Excuse me," Walter interjected, "before things are said that will be regretted, know this, Herr Kemper: whatever you think you know about me is wrong. What I do is recondite on purpose. Whatever you believe you can do to me, you can't. I'm *no one's* lickspittle. I can't do what you're asking of me." Walter paused. "However, I do have a suggestion. Move to Berlin."

"Berlin? Are you crazy?" Helmet said, bewildered.

"A month back, a protest in Berlin started with just a few people, people whose Jewish spouses had been arrested as a prelude to being sent to the camps. Over one week the protest grew until thousands of people were taking part. The SD, the SS Intelligence Service, wanted to kill all the protesters, but Herr Goebbels said no; at least that's my understanding. He said the protest concerned family matters and was not political, but it could turn political and spread throughout Germany if it continued. The spouses should be released unless they had committed a real crime. They were released. Instructions went out afterward that Jewish spouses were to be left alone."

"I don't believe you. That hasn't been in the news," Helmut challenged.

"If you were living in Sweden or listening to the BBC, you would be aware of it. The protest was called the Rosenstrassee protest. A remarkable thing. I expect a German married couple with one Jewish partner would be as safe in Berlin as anywhere. And one more thing, Helmut. If you do get arrested, Clara will need to call me. There is a strong likelihood that I could get you released."

"How strong?"

"Almost a hundred percent."

"From a jail in Berlin?"

"*Especially* from a jail in Berlin. But I would need to know right away. If you had been sent on to one of the camps, I could still help—possibly—but it would be much more difficult."

"Herr Last," Clara asked, "would it be safe to stay here in Cologne?"

"Perhaps, but I expect that the orders to leave Jewish spouses alone are more likely to be followed in Berlin."

Helmut's face was downcast, and he was not pleased with

Walter's suggestion nor his unwillingness to help in the manner Helmut wished. Walter, however, wasn't going to risk his mission when he felt that Helmut was relatively safe.

Clara turned to her husband. "Helmut, given Herr Last's observations, we should consider his suggestion."

"At the moment I don't like it. I need to give it some thought."

"Helmut, you have my card. Call me anytime. However, we would need to speak cryptically as the phone lines have elephant ears."

Walter bid Clara and Helmut goodbye and was on his way.

Three Months Later at the Border Crossing—April 2, 1943

Walter pulled up to the border crossing and stopped as usual. He got out of his truck to deliver Elsa's plate of goodies. A black convertible Mercedes pulled alongside Walter's truck. It was as long as a train engine and just as loud. The top was down, and Walter recognized the occupant—SS-Obergruppenführer Reinhard Heydrich. He was considered the second most dangerous man in Germany after his boss, Reichsfuhrer Himmler. Herr Heydrich had worked his way up since 1934 when he had been appointed head of the Gestapo. Along the way he was appointed Chief of Security Police and the SD, and finally SS-Obergruppenführer. Another black Mercedes, one of regular size, slowed and stopped in front of Walter's truck, blocking the way. Four Gestapo got out and stood alongside the car. Herr Heydrich got out of his car too.

"Herr Last, I don't believe we've met. I'm SS-Obergruppenführer Reinhard Heydrich."

"You're correct; we haven't met," Walter said as he held out his hand to shake rather than give the Nazi salute. Herr Heydrich smiled a tad at that. Walter had heard that Heydrich often overlooked a person's indiscretions if he thought the person could be useful to him, but he had no idea if that was true.

"Herr Last, I hear things about you—interesting things. I decided to see for myself."

"And just what is it I can do for you?"

"Open your truck."

Walter kept a business look on his face, no smile but a seeming lack of concern.

"Certainly. If you would, tell the border guards to go inside the station office as we conduct our business. I wouldn't want them to know what's in the truck you understand."

"Yes," Herr Heydrich agreed. He shouted orders to the border guards, and they walked to the border patrol station a few meters in front of the truck. Walter unlocked the back of the truck.

Before he opened it to reveal the contents, Walter turned to Herr Heydrich. "If you find something you like, take it. But only one, please, and leave me to my business."

Herr Heydrich nodded.

Walter hated to do this; it made him sick. But he could think of no other way to save the rest of the *contraband*.

Herr Heydrich walked over to his driver, told him to put up the top on his Mercedes, and walked back to the truck.

Walter opened the truck.

Herr Heydrich glanced at the *contraband*, then over to Walter before he pulled himself into the truck.

Walter walked over to the Mercedes, leaned against it, and watched.

Herr Heydrich found something to his liking and got out with it. He brought it over to his car, and as he was about to open the back door, he looked at Walter.

"I suppose I should ask first," Herr Heydrich said. He turned around, bowed slightly, and as if talking to a real live princess, said, "My dear, wouldn't you rather ride with me in this fine automobile instead of that closed-in, musty truck?"

Apparently the answer was yes. It was rumored that Herr Heydrich had a sense of humor. He opened the back door and deposited the *contraband*.

"I'll leave you to your business," he said to Walter. He walked around the car, got into the back seat with the princess, and drove away.

The Gestapo men got into their car and followed.

Walter walked over to his truck, but before he closed the back door, he said to the remaining *contraband*, "I'm ashamed of that, but there was no alternative. The rest of you will be safe now."

Walter went to the patrol station and told the guards that everything was okay. Then he proceeded into Switzerland.

At the Border Crossing—April 21, 1943

As Walter was getting closer to the border crossing, he saw a large Mercedes in the distance. He knew it was SS-Obergruppenführer Reinhard Heydrich. If Walter turned back now or tried to run, he'd lose. He noticed a small infantry truck with some SS men holding machine guns, and as he pulled to a stop and got out of his truck, the SS men surrounded his vehicle. Walter assumed Herr Heydrich wanted to conduct business again and take more *contraband*. The border guards were at their usual stations as Herr Heydrich didn't seem worried about them seeing what was in the truck this time. *Why?*

"So, Herr Last, we meet again—and so soon."

"You want another item from my truck?"

"No, Herr Last. I want the truck; I'm taking it."

"No, SS-Obergruppenführer Reinhard Heydrich, you're not." By using his full title, Walter wanted to emphasize to Herr Heydrich that despite his power, he was out of his depth.

Herr Heydrich raised his arm, and the SS men raised their machine guns. The border guards looked on, unsure.

"Herr Last, this is what will happen if I leave here without the truck. I know all about you rescuing Reichsfuhrer Himmler from a river when he was a boy and obtaining a warrant disc from him. Next week there will be a high-level meeting at the Berghof that will include many high-ranking officials, including Reichsfuhrer Himmler and me. I will confront Reichsfuhrer Himmler in front of the Führer and the others. The Führer will have no choice but to remove Reichsfuhrer Himmler when he finds out what you are doing and that Himmler has been protecting you. Then I will be promoted in his stead, and your protection will be gone. I don't believe that you have a choice."

"I wish I could be at Berchtesgaden for that meeting."

"I can arrange it."

"Tell me, are you required to hand over your weapons when in the presence of the Führer?"

"Of course; we all are."

"Well, Obergruppenführer Heydrich, if I attend the meeting, I will be allowed to keep my Luger; I won't have to hand it over. You see, *Adolf Hitler* was the little boy I rescued, not

Himmler. *Adolf Hitler* is the one who secured my warrant disc, not Himmler. *Adolf Hitler* is the one who gave me the number five, not Himmler. And if you doubt me, I suggest we call the Führer right now." Walter proceeded to call out Hitler's phone number.

The smile left Herr Heydrich's face. A look of doubt and reflection appeared. Then he smiled and nodded his head slightly.

"Herr Last, I'd like you to come work for me; but then . . . I suppose you wouldn't, considering what you have been doing these past few years."

He signaled for the SS men to lower their machine guns. He got in his car and drove off, followed by the truck with the SS men.

The border guards were relieved but unsure of what to make of the exchange. Walter was confident of one thing: his facing down SS-Obergruppenführer Reinhard Heydrich would give him all the vitamin B he would ever need, at least at the border crossing. Walter got into his truck, the border guards lifted the gate, and he was on his way. He thought about what Elsa had said to him once, "Walter, you can lie like nobody's business if you have to."

Passing through the Swiss border was no problem. Walter was en route to the drop-off location for the *contraband* when he stopped at a small out-of-the-way church. He had grown up with the man who was the priest there. The priest agreed to help Walter with certain matters, although he didn't know exactly what Walter was doing. He didn't want to know. Walter preferred it that way too. Occasionally Walter would end up with a dead body mixed in with the *contraband*. When this did happen, he would stop at the church, and his friend would take the body and give the person or persons a Christian burial. Walter didn't know if that was the right thing to do—a Christian burial—in light of whom these people were. But considering all the evil in the world at that moment, he thought he could be forgiven for it.

Sometime in April 1945—
A few weeks before Germany Surrendered

Walter pulled up to the border crossing. There had been reports of American soldiers in the area. All the border guards had thrown their guns into the river, but they were still performing their duties. Hans brought Walter a cup of so-called coffee. Walter sat down on a bench to drink his coffee. Hans sat too and wolfed down some of Elsa's treats. Walter was finishing his coffee when one of the border guards started shouting and pointing. Hans and Walter ran over to see what the commotion was. They saw an American jeep and several troop trucks speeding to the border. All the border guards lined up with their hands on their heads as the Americans pulled up. A captain got out of the jeep. The soldiers in the troop trucks jumped down and started frisking the guards. Walter was the only one without his hands on his head.

The captain walked up to Walter while one of the American soldiers had a gun trained on him.

"You speak English?" the captain asked.

"Yes, some," Walter replied.

"Is this your truck?"

"Yes, I was about to cross the border into Switzerland."

"Empty your pockets."

"I will, very slowly. I have a Luger and a Gestapo warrant

disc on me."

A colt pistol was now pointing at Walter too. The captain quickly pulled it from his holster. "Yes, very slowly."

One of the soldiers walked up to Walter and took his Luger, then his warrant disc.

"What is your name?" the captain asked.

"Walter Last."

"Well, Herr Last, open the truck; let's have a look."

Walter unlocked the back of the truck, opened it, and took a few steps back.

The captain walked up to the truck and whistled.

"Wow," the captain said as he hopped into the truck. He took a minute or two looking around. Then he hopped out. "You know there's a dead body in there?"

Walter nodded.

"This gold, furniture, paintings, and other items must be worth thousands of dollars, maybe more. I imagine you killed the SS man in there, then stole all this from the Nazis who stole it from the Jews given that there is an itemized list of everything with what looks like mostly Jewish names and their addresses. Planning to cross the border with the loot before we got here, I bet."

"All of this belongs to the Jews, Captain, except the SS man."

"Walter Last, we're going to take you in."

The captain took a rifle from one of his men and started to walk away, but he quickly turned and thrust the butt of the gun into Walter's stomach.

Walter doubled over; the wind knocked out of him.

"You *disgust me*, Walter Last."

Within a minute another jeep pulled up. The tag on the front had one star, an American general's jeep. As the general stepped out, all the American soldiers stood at attention and saluted. By then Walter was standing up straight. The general told the soldiers to be at ease. He plopped down on the hood of his jeep, looked at Walter, and smiled.

Walter smiled back.

"So, Captain, what is going on here?"

"Sir, this man Walter Last is trying to get into Switzerland. It looks as if he killed an SS officer and took valuables that were stolen from Jewish families."

"And what does Herr Last say about this?"

"I haven't asked him, sir. It seems pretty clear what's going on."

"Let's hear what he has to say anyway. Herr Last, if you please."

"Certainly." Walter had finally caught his breath. "For eight years I have brought Jewish property that the Nazis had stolen or were going to steal from Jewish families to a warehouse in Switzerland. All the property has been cataloged with the names and addresses of the families it belonged to. At some point—I hope—the property can be returned. The Swiss Federal Council is aware of what I'm doing. I can explain how I was able to collect this property, if necessary."

"And you've never kept or lost any of these items you've collected?" the general asked.

"Well..."

"Go on, Herr Last. You're among friends here."

"There was one item I let SS-Obergruppenführer Reinhard Heydrich take as a bribe so that the others could continue on their journey—and to save my life and my mission, I expect."

"And what was this item?"

"It was *Princess Pauline Sander Metternich*, the painting by Franz Xavier Winterhalter."

"Um . . . and the dead German . . . what about him?"

"At times some of my friends came across Nazis who died under mysterious circumstances—usually involving bullet holes. If the bodies weren't discovered, the authorities would have no reason to expect foul play. After all, the person could have been killed in an air raid or have disappeared on their own. But if the bodies were discovered, innocent people would have been rounded up and executed to set an example. To keep that from happening, I took the bodies into Switzerland for burial. The Swiss Federal Council is not aware I am doing this."

"In that case, your secret is safe with us. Go ahead and cross the border," the general said.

"General," the captain shouted, "surely you're not going to believe this canard from this man?"

"I do believe this man, Captain. Herr Last is my father. Hello, Dad."

"Hello, son. Your mother has been repining to see you and waiting for this war to end. I have one question . . . considering all the Enigma codes I sent the Americans, what the hell took you so long?"

The End

3
Too Much Trouble

Monday

My investigation started out easier than I had expected. I didn't have to cajole, entice, or hagride Earl Pardee—what luck. I called Mr. Pardee, a vice president at the Northern & Southern National Bank, feigning that I was a stockbroker.

"Hello, Mr. Pardee, this is Wagner Wheeler. I'm a stockbroker and would like to offer you some once-in-a-lifetime investment opportunities. The president of the bank, Mr. Jackson-Monroe, can vouch for me. Can we set up a meeting?" He didn't pick up on the incongruity of *some* rather than *a* with the phrase "once-in-a-lifetime."

"Well, this certainly is fortuitous," Mr. Pardee replied. "I expect to come into some money any day now, and I certainly want above-average returns so I can quit this crummy job. Tomorrow is a bank holiday. Can you come by my house tomorrow morning, say ten?"

"I can. What's the address?" I asked, even though I knew it.

"I'm at 201 West First Street."

"Fine. I'll see you tomorrow."

My boss, Mr. Daniels, had given me the assignment and a file on Mr. Pardee. I knew that he would not ask Mr. Jackson-Monroe about me as the file indicated that Mr. Pardee despised Mr. Jackson-Monroe. And even if Mr. Pardee did ask, he couldn't be sure that Mr. Jackson-Monroe would be frank.

Tuesday

I was getting dressed for my meeting with Mr. Pardee. As I rummaged around in my dresser, I found my ID:

Federal Deposit Insurance Corporation
FDIC Office of Inspector General
OIG Special Agent

I didn't expect to need it, but I took it anyway. I also had a gun, but I usually left it locked up after what had happened on my first case many years earlier. I had entered Mrs. Mason's kitchen, which, for a reason she hadn't explained, featured metal detectors at each doorway. So I put the gun on a table. Mrs. Mason grabbed it and acted out a scene from *Bonnie and Clyde* when she discharged the weapon. The bullet hit Daisy in the midsection.

Mrs. Mason glanced at Daisy, shrugged her shoulders, and said, "Oh well, Daisy always was shamelessly seedy." Good thing for all concerned that Daisy was just that—a daisy, a flower. Yes, Mrs. Mason named her plants. She said Daisy needed pruning anyway. After that incident I thought it best to leave the sidearm locked up at the office.

An hour later I was on the sidewalk of West First Street looking for 201. The address was only a few blocks from my house, so I walked. But West First Street wasn't a street I ventured down often simply because I had no reason to. It wasn't because I was suspicious like other folks: suspicious of the sewage plant (alleged), the asylum (alleged), and the POW camp from World War I (alleged), all of which were farther down the street and long since abandoned. I say *alleged* because what those facilities had been people assumed because of something the town gossip had said years ago, which kept getting repeated. It was kind of like the grammar "rule" that you use the word *fewer*, not the word *less*, with count nouns (chair is a count noun, furniture is not)—except for the exceptions, of course. And all because Robert Baker wrote a book in 1770 saying, in effect, that the word *fewer* sounded better to him with count nouns than the word *less*. But that wasn't a rule then, and he didn't say it should be a rule, but umpteen people since have.

The neighborhood looked the same as mine: middle-class homes, well-kept yards, mature trees—a typical setting that you might see on TV or in the movies. The houses had mostly been built in the 1920s, creating a neighborhood like Charlie Newton (Teresa Wright) lived in on *Shadow of a Doubt*.

I noticed activity a bit farther down the street. A delivery truck had backed into someone's driveway. As I approached, I watched a grandfather clock on a hand truck being guided through the front door of a house. Once I reached the house, I realized it was the home of Earl Pardee. When I arrived at the front door, I had to step aside to let the delivery man back out of the house with the grandfather clock on the hand truck. Perhaps they brought Mr. Pardee the wrong clock. In any case, I rang the doorbell.

A soigné woman around forty answered the door. You know the type, well dressed, not a hair out of place, with a face that exuded intelligence. "Yes, may I have your name?"

"Well, I suppose," I responded, "but it's not the most suitable name for a woman."

She looked at me blankly, making no attempt to appear even slightly amused. If the house had had a servant's entrance, she would have told me to use it. She patiently stood there regarding me. Perhaps she wondered if I had escaped from the long-since-abandoned (alleged) asylum.

"Wagner Wheeler. I have an appointment to see Mr. Earl Pardee."

At that, a boy riding his bike on the sidewalk shouted, "Good morning, Mrs. Pardee."

Mrs. Pardee looked up and shouted back, "Good morning, Jonny," as she waved.

"Follow me," Mrs. Pardee said. "Wait here if you please." She pointed to the living room off to the right.

I noticed a pencil on the living room carpet and reached down to pick it up, but Mrs. Pardee said, "Ah . . . leave that alone; don't touch a thing. I'll tell Earl you're here." She disappeared down the hall.

A man was adjusting the grandfather clock that stood against the wall in the hallway, so I said, "I thought y'all just took out a grandfather clock?"

"We did. This is the one we brought in."

"The other one is broken?"

"Nope. It just had the wrong time—standard time. This one has daylight saving time."

What the heck, I wondered, Was I still asleep? I couldn't leave it alone; I had to ask, "Couldn't you just change the time?"

"*Too much trouble*; at least that's Mr. Pardee's thought on the matter. Gives us business though. We store his clocks and change them out twice a year when the time changes. Of course we reset any clocks that stop while in storage."

"And he pays for that?"

"Nah, the city does."

"Our city . . . Amville pays for it?"

"Yep, for the storage and our labor to move the clocks in and out. And we change out all the clocks—even change out the oven since there's a clock in it."

"Sheesh! Is Pardee on the city council or something?"

"Nope, says there's some kind of state law that the city has to pay for it. You need to ask him if you want to know exactly."

"I certainly will." I turned, went into the living room, and sat down. There were quite a few things scattered about on the carpet. But after Mrs. Pardee's admonishment, I wasn't touching a thing.

After a few minutes Mr. Pardee came into the living room, and introductions were exchanged. He insisted we use first names and asked me to follow him to his study. After we entered the study, he closed the door.

"As I mentioned on the phone yesterday, Wagner, I expect to come into some money and want to put it into stocks that will explode like gangbusters. Of course I also want little risk."

Yeah, as if a broker never hears that. He might as well have asked me to take the LSAT exam while bareback bronc riding with a monkey on my back, the Hope diamond balanced on my head, whilst holding the entire fourteen-book Bernard Gunter series in one hand.

"Earl, how much money are we talking about, and how soon will you have it?"

"Follow me."

We walked through the house to the unattached garage and stood behind his car while he opened the trunk.

"What do you see?" Earl asked.

"A large white duffle bag with the words US Dollars stenciled on it."

"That's right. There is one hundred fifty thousand dollars in that bag."

Earl closed the trunk and we walked back to his study.

"The whole point of that exercise was to give you an example of how money seems to come my way. But in this case, the money is not mine. It's only there due to banking regulations."

"Banking regulations?"

"Yes. I don't expect you to know this, Wagner, but banks are only allowed to keep so much cash. If the bank's cash is over the FDIC limit at the end of the day, we must take the excess to another bank. That happened to be the case yesterday. By the time I arrived at the Great Eastern & Western Bank, it was closed, so I had to bring the money home. And that's not the first time that's happened, believe you me. And since I'm a notaphilist, I often look through the bag for valuable bills, and trade. Occasionally it can be a day or two before I get the money back to the bank."

Of course I knew that FDIC regulation. I also knew Earl was breaking the law, big time. It startled me that he was so flippant about disclosing his indiscretion.

"You're not concerned that someone will steal the money?"

"Nah. Nobody even knows it's there. And this is a quiet neighborhood." Then, in a hushed tone, Earl continued, "I expect a large inheritance soon. But the situation is rather delicate, and it's best that Mrs. Pardee not know of this."

"I see. Can you give me more details regarding the amount and the timing?"

Before he could respond, we heard a knock on the study door.

"Come in," Earl said.

Mrs. Pardee opened the door. She held a tray with two glasses of what I guessed was iced tea. Earl sat at his desk and made a few notes while I sat on the other side. Mrs. Pardee set the tray down and brought us each a glass.

When she turned to leave, Earl said, "Ah, Sapphire, who was that I saw you with at the café on Elm Street yesterday?"

"You know exactly who it was—Mike Fracks."

"Two months ago, when I saw you two together, you told me Mike was a quondam lover; that's why I was surprised to see you with him again."

"I did say that; that's true. But I meant quondam in the sense of sometimes, not in the sense of former."

"I've asked you before not to use contronyms with me."

"I'm not sure quondam is a contronym. And in light of your response to my comments two months ago when you came into the café, I thought you *tempered* your attitude toward Mike and that you were *sanctioning* our relationship. Your discursive comments *cleaved* Mike and me. I thought then that my relationship with Mike would be a matter of your *oversight*. And I decided to fight *with* him, and rightly so as your behavior made you look like a cuckolded husband. Of course . . . dear . . . we probably shouldn't be having this conversation in front of our guest. Despite the trophies on the wall, he probably doesn't know you're a great *nimrod*. We may be flummoxing him." Sapphire turned and left, closing the door on her way out.

Earl sighed and kept writing.

I had a tough time forfending a laugh. I counted six contronyms—including *with* (was her fight against [with] Mike or with Mike against Earl)—and I wasn't even counting quondam. Mrs. Pardee—Sapphire—was undeniably more elfin than I expected; suddenly I liked her. Not one in ten thousand people know what contronyms are, much less have the ability to use them on the fly as she did.

"You'll have to forgive Sapphire, Wagner. Sometimes she acts untoward. But back to our business. I expect to inherit ten million or so very soon."

"I see . . . one of your relatives?"

"Not exactly. Sapphire's uncle is expected to go any day now."

"You're in his will?"

"In the will, no—everything goes to Sapphire. He never married and other relations are well-off. But I convinced him to sign a POD form listing me as the sole beneficiary of all his investment accounts, which are the majority of his assets. He might have been confused about what the POD form was for. And I got someone I know who drinks too much to notarize it."

I couldn't believe Earl was telling me this too. A POD (payable on death) form transfers the assets to a beneficiary after a person's death. The assets would not go through probate and would not be included in the estate; therefore, the provisions of the will would not apply.

"But of course this will benefit you too, Wagner. A good deal for us both, I'd say."

"It certainly is," I replied. But that wasn't why I was there. I needed to determine if he was taking funds from the bank. And that money in his trunk qualified, not to mention the fact that he had done it before. I had recorded our conversation and taken pictures of his car's trunk with a camera hidden in my shirt button.

Then came another knock on the office door.

"Come in," Earl said.

Sapphire opened the door and said, "Earl, the yard man is

here. Didn't you want to discuss a few things with him?"

"Yes. Excuse me for a few minutes, Wagner. I need to take care of this." And Earl left the room.

"Mr. Wheeler, may I get you more to drink?"

"Call me Wagner, please. And no thank you, I'm fine."

"Well, Wagner Please, you can call me Sapphire You're Welcome."

I cachinnated at that.

"You're something else, aren't you, Sapphire You're Welcome?"

"Quite. So why are you here?"

"I'm a stockbroker looking for some business."

"Really?"

"Yes."

"Oh, please. I don't think so."

"Excuse me?"

"What is the current PE ratio of the S&P 500?"

"Ah . . ."

"Or the current yield on the ten-year treasury bill?"

"It's been a while since I—"

"You don't have to tell me, Wagner Please, but I'm confident you're not a stockbroker. You must be investigating Earl. Oh, don't worry; I'm not going to tell. Earl's not one of my favorite people."

"Sapphire—"

"Don't lie anymore; it may tarnish my impression of you."

With alacrity I decided to change the subject, so I said, "You and Earl certainly have a unique way of handling daylight saving time."

Sapphire laughed. "Hardly. Earl's method is the stupidest way of handling it that I can imagine. It makes it harder on me, somewhat."

"Oh?"

"Yes, who wouldn't want to handle the time change correctly, the way I do."

"You mean changing the clocks twice a year as everybody else does?"

"Good heavens—of course not—Wagner Please. Changing the time back and forth is just plain stupid. I *never* change the time on my watch or my clocks. I stay on standard time all year. Doctors, sleep scientists, and the like agree that standard time is correlated to the human body's circadian rhythm and that the human body never adjusts to daylight saving time."

The Pardees were an interesting bunch.

"That must get confusing," I said.

"Most of the time, no. I adapted to it expeditiously. If my doctor's appointment is at four, I know to put it in my calendar as three. And if a show I want to watch comes on at ten, I just remember it's nine. That's what I do while daylight saving time is in effect. You'd be amazed at how quickly you can adjust. Isn't there something, some habit you changed that was much easier than you figured it would be?"

"Verily, there is: putting one space after a period instead of two. I went years, perhaps decades, not realizing that using two spaces was wrong, which it has been ever since computers replaced typewriters. At first I thought I was too old to change, that I wouldn't be able to. Even some members of the University of Chicago Press, which produces the *Chicago Manual of Style,* haven't changed for that reason. But I tried, and after only two days I was typing without having to stop and backspace. I think you're on to something there, Sapphire."

"I'm on to a lot of things, Wagner Please." She gave me a roguish grin.

As we continued bantering, we inched closer and closer toward each other as if we were magnets set to attract. Ultimately our faces were only inches apart. We heard Earl's footsteps in the hallway, and we both took a few steps back.

"I'll let you two get back to it," Sapphire said as Earl stepped into the room. She closed the door behind her.

"Earl, if you don't mind my asking, the city pays for you to store your clocks and change them out twice a year?"

"Yep."

"Why is that?"

"State law. The law says that if the state government has a law on the books that there is no rational reason for, and it creates an expense for a citizen, the person's city of residence must reimburse the individual for the expense. At first the city refused to pay, so I sued, and the case went all the way up to the state supreme court. The court didn't want to agree with me, but since the state can change the law and not recognize daylight saving time—without requiring approval from the US Congress by the way—it is, in fact, causing me to incur an expense for no rational reason. The fact that I hired a storage company to handle the matter wasn't at issue."

"Good gosh. How would you even know about that law?"

"My great-uncle, Clarence. When he got older, he needed a cane, but he still wobbled when he walked. It's against the law to step on frogs on the sidewalk. With all of Clarence's wobbling, he stepped on frogs and kept getting fined. He was a retired lawyer and knew about that specific law, so he hired a couple of full-time nurses to walk with him to keep him from stepping on frogs, and the city had to pay for them."

"Holy cow!"

"Yeah, and since that's the law, why not take advantage of it. But anent our business, let's get together in another day or two and make final arrangements."

"Sounds fine. Can you give me a list of the assets you'll inherit, so I can start planning?"

"Sure. As a matter of fact, I have a copy of my uncle-in-law's brokerage statement that you can have." He opened the desk drawer, pulled out the statement, and handed it to me. I put it in my briefcase.

"Thanks for your time. I'm sure we'll have a profitable partnership."

Earl walked me to the front door, we shook hands, and I left.

Just as I got to the sidewalk, Sapphire came around the side of the house and called out. "Wagner Please, one moment."

I stopped as Sapphire ambled over.

"Earl wants me to ask if you could come back tomorrow morning at ten thirty?"

"I thought he would be working tomorrow."

"He is but not until later in the day."

"Okay. Maybe I'll see you tomorrow too."

"Mayhap you will."

I smiled and sauntered off. Sapphire smiled too.

After I got home, I drove to the office. Inside, I saw Mr. Daniels in the hall.

"How's the Pardee thing going?" he asked.

"Very well."

"Anything to it?"

"Yes. You'll have my report by the end of the day. No question, Mr. Pardee can be arrested."

"Okay, I'll set up an appointment with Mr. Lane, the district attorney; Mr. Jackson-Monroe, the bank president; and Mr. Rossi, the head of the FDIC, for tomorrow afternoon."

"Fine."

When I reached my office, I unloaded the Pardee files and the brokerage statement that Earl had given me. I typed up my notes, conducted some research online, and printed a thing or two. I reviewed the uncle's brokerage statement to get an idea of exactly what investments he owned, completed some paperwork, and organized all my material. Then I prepared my recordings and pictures from my visit with Earl. I packed all my Pardee material into my briefcase, dropped off a copy of my report at Mr. Daniels's office, and headed home.

Wednesday

I rang the bell at the Pardee house at ten thirty. I had walked again.

"Why, Wagner Please, how nice of you to stop by," Sapphire said when she answered the door.

I gazed at her with an expression that asked, *Are you going to keep calling me that*?

As if reading my thoughts, Sapphire said, "Yes, I am going to keep calling you that."

That was okay with me; I liked it.

"I'm here to see Earl as he requested."

"He's at work."

I closed my eyes, tilted my head, then opened my eyes, staring her square in the eyes. "So that's how it's going to be, is it?"

"He's sorry. Something came up. He'll call you later."

"Is that so?"

"Surely you don't think I'd lie, Wagner Please."

Her expression and the way she was dressed intimated that she was lying. She wore a tight white knit dress that ended a few inches above her knees, white high-heel sandals, red lipstick, and enough jewelry to sink the *Queen Mary*. She must have spent at least an hour on her curly and bouncy hairdo. A good thing rain wasn't forecast.

"I need to do a few things today, Wagner Please. I thought you could accompany me."

"Aren't you afraid of getting robbed wearing all that jewelry?"

"It's all fake. Earl won't buy me the real stuff. But I wear it because it keeps men away."

"Oh?"

"It makes them think I'm high maintenance."

"Doesn't the wedding ring keep men away?"

"Not in this town."

"So what are *we* doing today, Sapphire?"

"Well, I want to visit my uncle in the nursing home. Then we can have lunch at the country club. My uncle lets me use his membership. And if you're interested, we could play tennis after."

"Wearing those shoes?"

"I'll change, silly man."

"Okay, I'll call my office and be ready in a minute."

"Why?"

"Why what?"

"Why do you have to call the office?"

"SEC compliance. Brokerage firms keep a record of places brokers go while they're working." It wasn't an SEC rule; I needed to speak with Marvin Belford at the office. I couldn't believe my luck—second time in three days.

"SEC, brokerage firm . . . you're still playing that game. Okay, I won't cramp your style. I'll be out in a jiffy."

The upscale nursing home was bright with large rooms and impressive amenities. Uncle Bernie was propped up in bed, and we sat next to him. He was coherent at times, drifted off at times, and rambled at times. When he drifted off, Sapphire and I bantered as we seemed to be in the habit of doing.

"Wagner Please, I need to talk to the administrator. You okay if I leave you with Uncle Bernie for a few minutes?"

"Yeah, I'll be fine."

Sapphire returned about ten minutes later.

"I need to use the restroom," I said.

"Okay, it's time to go anyway. I'll meet you by the front door."

I nodded, picked up my briefcase, and left. Marvin came over and started a conversation while I was waiting by the front door. As soon as he saw Sapphire, he shook my hand and left.

"Who was that?" Sapphire asked.

"Marvin Belford. He works in the same office I do. He has a great-aunt here."

Sapphire and I had lunch at the country club, but I told her no tennis because I needed to be back in the office for an appointment. She dropped me off at my house. I realized later, I hadn't given her my address.

I headed to the office. On the way, I made one stop.

The meeting with Mr. Lane, Mr. Jackson-Monroe, Mr. Daniels, Mr. Rossi, and me ended at three thirty. All agreed that Earl Pardee was going to jail. Mr. Rossi wanted the maximum sentence—twenty years. He said that an example needed to be set. Mr. Lane reluctantly agreed. We figured to wait until Thursday afternoon, when Earl returned home from work, to arrest him. There was no reason to think that Earl would run before then. I told the gathering I could think of millions of reasons he wouldn't. Besides, I had a meeting scheduled with Earl for eight the following morning.

I finished a few odds and ends before leaving the office. On Wednesdays I always treated myself to dinner out. I would stop by The Hellenic on the way home. It was an inviting place, a bit upscale, and served more than just Greek food. A shirt and tie was expected. Since I ate there weekly, the owner, Maximos, always had a table ready for me. I arrived just after five.

"Ah, good afternoon, Wagner. Nice to see you as always. Your table is waiting and your guest has arrived."

"Guest?"

"Yes. And very redoubtable she is."

I knew right away who it was and let out a short laugh at Maximos's description—*redoubtable*. Not quite a contronym, yet both definitions—causing fear or worthy of respect—could apply to my dinner companion.

"I must say," Maximos continued, "I approve. Few women—few people at all—know about the 1827 Naval Battle of Navarino, which ensured Greek independence from the Ottoman Empire. And I must say, we Europeans are more tolerant of these matters than you Americans seem to be."

"Tolerant?"

"Yes, you know." Maximos held up his left hand and pointed to his fourth finger with the wedding ring.

"She's just a friend, Maximos."

He wrinkled his nose, nodded, and said, "Of course... *bon appétit.*"

I strode over to my table where Sapphire was studying the menu.

"Good afternoon, Sapphire."

"Good afternoon, Wagner Please."

"So you know where I eat supper on Wednesdays?"

"Clearly."

"And where I live?"

"Seems so. I'm a bit of a detective myself."

I pulled out a chair and sat down.

"Aren't you concerned Earl might see us together?"

"No. Tonight is poker night at Jack Smith's place. And I wouldn't be surprised if Earl isn't in prison soon. Then he'll be unable to do anything about my assignations."

Sapphire was a bold woman.

"Tell me, what do you do when you're not working?"

She wore the sweetest expression, kinda like she really wanted to know.

"Read, write short stories, diagram sentences, listen to music, watch old movies, and other assorted odds and ends."

"What do you read?"

"Nonfiction, fiction, grammar books."

"Grammar books, you say. Then let me ask you this: You're in the grocery store, in front of the checkout stations. The sign on the register reads Ten Items or Less. Should it say, Ten Items or Fewer?"

My heart fluttered.

"Some folks would say it should. But they would be wrong. People only believe that because of Robert—"

"Robert Baker and the book he wrote in 1770," Sapphire cut in.

A smile stuck on my face for the rest of the evening.

Thursday

Earl and I had been discussing investments and had just wrapped up our meeting when his phone rang.

"Excuse me a second," Earl said, taking the call. "Earl Pardee. Ah . . . yes . . . I see. Nothing more could have been done. No, no, I'm sure y'all did all you could. Thank you for letting me know. Yes, I'll let Mrs. Pardee know. Thank you."

Within a millisecond Earl was prancing around his desk, singing softly, "I'm a rich man now. I'm a rich man now, la-lala-la-lala." This went on for two minutes.

"Sorry, Wagner. I'm just so, so happy. And you too, I'm sure. I'm sad he's gone, of course, but he had a long life, and it was his time. If you don't mind, considering our deal is arranged, I'll call you in a week or so once his assets are transferred to me. But right now, I need to tell Sapphire."

"I understand. I'll see myself out."

I didn't see Sapphire on the way out. I had driven to Earl's for this visit, so I hopped into my car and headed to the office.

Earl, meanwhile, gave Sapphire the news and started his errands. His first stop was his uncle-in-law's brokerage firm.

"Hello, I'm Earl Pardee. I have a document to turn in. It's a form one of your clients recently signed; I'm afraid the gentleman has passed away."

"Oh, I'm sorry for your loss, Mr. Pardee. Was he a relative?"

"Yes, an uncle. Here's the form."

"Certainly, let me take a look. Everything appears to be in order. Take this form, complete it, and bring it back in the next couple of days. Once we get the death certificate, we can transfer the investments to you within two or three days. How does that sound?"

"Fine."

"Let me put this in your uncle's file, then I'll give you a receipt for the POD form."

"Okay."

A minute later the woman returned.

"Here's your uncle's file. Let me put this in the . . . oh, what's this? Wait a minute." The woman pulled a document out of the file and started reading it.

"Is something wrong?" Earl asked.

"Well, yes. The POD document you gave me isn't valid."

"But you just told me it was in order."

"Yes, it is. But your POD is dated two weeks ago."

"So?"

"We have another POD form dated yesterday, so yours is no longer valid."

"What? That . . . that can't be."

"I'm afraid it is."

"Who's the beneficiary?"

"Oh, I think you're in luck there, Mr. Pardee. It's Sapphire Pardee, your wife."

A rictus appeared on Earl's face, and he staggered to a chair.

"Who . . . who brought in that POD form?" Earl asked.

"Let's see. I don't remember this one." The woman turned and called out, "Suzy, can you come here a minute?"

A woman who looked like Essie Davis with a bob haircut came over.

"Yes?"

"Do you remember who brought this POD form in?"

Suzy studied the form.

"Oh, yes. I remember him . . . such a witty guy."

"What was his name?"

"Wheeler . . . Wagner Wheeler."

Earl Pardee was arrested at his home that afternoon. He confessed and told the police about all the times he had taken money home. He appeared distraught and didn't seem to care about going to jail.

Friday

Yeah, Earl had only been arrested yesterday, and maybe I was being a cad. But what an opportunity for me! I liked Sapphire, and she had agreed to meet me for dinner at Steaks Galore on Sixth Street at four. I was in the lobby of our office heading for my rendezvous with Sapphire when I ran into Mr. Jackson-Monroe, president of the Northern and Southern National Bank.

"Oh, good afternoon, Mr. Jackson-Monroe."

"Hello, Mr. Wheeler."

"You here paying your bill?"

"Paying my bill?"

"Yes, for the Earl Pardee investigation."

"Well, no. That wasn't an investigation we asked for. We had no idea Earl was committing any crimes."

"Really? Who then?" I asked with a puzzled expression.

"I don't know. I assumed the FDIC hired you. They do that on occasion, hire private investigators because they are short-staffed."

"I see. Yes, you're probably right; the FDIC must have hired us."

Mr. Jackson-Monroe turned and left the building.

"You leaving for the day, Wagner?" asked Gloria, the receptionist.

"In a few minutes. I need to see Alice in accounting first. Oh, yeah. Here is an FDIC ID Mr. Daniels gave me to use on the Pardee investigation. Bill asked me for it. Can you give it to him?"

Gloria nodded.

I headed down the hall to Alice's office. The door was open, so I knocked and walked in.

"Wagner, what can I do for you?"

"The bill for the Earl Pardee case. Who paid it?"

"You're in luck. The payment just came in. Let's see. Yes, here it is.

Alice picked up the check and handed it to me.

"Well, well. What do you know," I said to no one in particular. I gave the check back to Alice. I was going over to see Mr. Daniels when I bumped into him in the hall.

"Sorry, Mr. Daniels."

"Quite all right. Were you coming to see me?"

"Yes. Why did you assign me to the Earl Pardee case?"

"Mrs. Pardee requested you."

"She did?"

"Yes."

"Why?"

"She didn't say."

"Okay, thanks."

"Sure."

When I arrived at Steaks Galore, Sapphire was already there, so I joined her.

"Good afternoon, Mrs. Pardee."

"Mrs. Pardee . . . have I done something wrong?" Sapphire asked as she winked at me.

"Good afternoon, Sapphire."

"That's better. I need to thank you, Wagner Please."

"Nothing to thank me for inasmuch as you were paying for it."

"Well, yes and no. I knew Earl had thousands of dollars in his car now and again. That's why I hired the Pinkerton Agency and you. But I knew nothing about the POD form until earlier today when Bernie's brokerage firm told me what had happened. That's why Marvin Belford was at the nursing home—not to see his great-aunt but to notarize the POD form you had Uncle Bernie sign listing me as the beneficiary. That's why I'm thanking you."

"You're welcome. Why did you ask Mr. Daniels to assign me to the case?"

"Emerald Wilson is my sister."

"I see."

Emerald Wilson had been kidnapped the year before. The ransom payoff, which I was handling, went wrong or started to. I had to step in front of a bullet that was heading for Emerald, saving her life. Fortunately, the Hewlett Packard 12C financial calculator in my shirt pocket stopped the bullet. I have a few calculators, so no great loss. The force jolted me, but I recovered quickly and jumped on the kidnapper as he attempted to absquatulate—case closed. I got a good bonus. Mr. Daniels rarely paid bonuses, but he loved good publicity.

"I've had all Earl's stuff packed up and put in storage. The house is in my name, so that's not a problem. I'm buying new furniture. Mayhap you'd like to come with me to pick it out."

"Oh."

"Yes, it's important for me to know what you like. I thought perhaps you'd move in with me."

"Earl might not like that."

"He'll be in prison for twenty years, so I don't think that matters. And it's not like he's my husband; he's only a brother-in-law."

"Where's your husband? That information wasn't in the report."

"He died."

"I'm sorry."

"Me too."

"What happened?"

"Earl killed him, but I can't prove it. Maybe you can help me with that too."

"Maybe I can."

The End

4
The Letters from the Train

In the state of . . . in the United States of America, if a married woman sleeps with an unmarried man and the injured party files a complaint, the pair can be charged with a felony. They each can be sentenced to four years in prison. Bryant Jackson knows that. Just a compelling observation you understand.

Dreams tormented Maxwell for days, and they always ended with the woman being led away in handcuffs. The dreams were triggered by something illicit he had seen on July 9. It was unbearable. He had to do something. He wanted the man to go to jail but not the woman. The woman had kept his parents from losing their house during the Depression, mislaying the foreclosure papers and hiding them from her husband, the sheriff. She often helped people surreptitiously. But the man she was involved with—Maxwell didn't care about the man. He deserved to be punished. He had, no doubt, led her astray. But if the man were punished, she would be too, unless Maxwell could finagle things just so. He came up with a plan. It wasn't the perfect solution, but at least it would keep her from going to prison.

"Yes, Maxwell," said Serenity, "I did tell Phaedra you're here. She's such a girly girl that it takes her forever to get done up—a trait I'd think you'd find unappealing, especially since this happens all the time. It's your move by the way."

Maxwell looked down at the chessboard. He couldn't recall ever seeing Phaedra not done up. She was pleasing to the eye. He loved sitting across from her on the porch and watching her swing. However, half the time he wasn't listening to what she said as she was a bit of a chatterbox, so his mind wandered. Maxwell moved one of his chess pieces.

Serenity watched Maxwell's eyes while she slowly slid her queen across the board, stopping next to Maxwell's king. "Checkmate, silly boy."

"Bloody he—"

"Maxwell, Daddy doesn't like swearing."

"Sorry, your move surprised me. I missed it."

"You miss a lot."

"What are you talking about?"

Phaedra opened the front door and sashayed to the swing on the porch.

"Good morning, Maxwell. And thanks, dear sister, for keeping him entertained." Phaedra looked down at the board. "Chess, yuck. Why don't we go for a walk, Maxwell?"

"Sure, let me put the chess pieces away."

Phaedra walked gracefully to the sidewalk.

As Maxwell handed Serenity the last piece—the king—to put in the box, she clasped his hand and said, "The game depends on the king. He is necessary, yet so dependent on the queen's good graces to keep him out of snares. He's too timid. The king needs to boldly go where no man has gone before."

Serenity knew what was to become the most famous split infinitive in the world because Gene Roddenberry had lived next door for a few years while working on a TV script.

Maxwell held her gaze.

"Maxwell, come on," Phaedra called out impatiently.

Serenity let go of his hand, and Maxwell put the king back on the chessboard—not in the box.

"Where should the king go?"

Serenity picked up the king and said, "Where he belongs," and she put the king in the box—next to the queen.

As Phaedra and Maxwell strolled, Phaedra said, "We shouldn't have done what we did the other day . . . I mean, since we're not married and all."

"I suspect a lot of couples who aren't married do that."

"Maxwell, really. I would hope a couple would be engaged before that kind of kiss was planted on a woman's lips. What is it called, a French—"

"Perhaps you're right. Sorry."

"Sorry? You need to make this right. You know what I mean?"

"Can we talk about something else?"

"All right." Phaedra knew Maxwell could be shy about such matters, and she gave him a kiss. Astonishingly, it was the kind of kiss she had just been harping about, perhaps to prod him and reinforce that he needed to make it right.

Maxwell was in his mid-twenties and worked as a Railway Mail Service postal clerk on the Railway Post Office—a specially designed train car where post office employees sorted the mail. In the early 1950s, 93 percent of the nonlocal mail was moved by train. Few could pass the Railway Post Office entrance exam, but Maxwell had. The exam tested potential employees on the names and locations of thousands of towns in their section of the country, and applicants had to be able to sort 600 pieces of mail in under an hour. This task was not easy because most envelopes were addressed in cursive and lacked a zip code, which didn't come into use until the 1960s.

Bob and Stu were on this day's mail run with Maxwell. Bob was an old-timer with forty years of service and held many records, including fastest sorter, least missorted mail, and no demerits. Everyone wanted Bob on their run. Anent his speed, he would bring a book to read when he finished sorting. Even after his wife passed away several years back, he kept working because he noticed that many retired friends fell into disrepair rather quickly.

Stu was five years older than Maxwell but had only been a post office employee for a year. He was good enough at the job, but it wasn't his dream.

The train sputtered and coughed as it came to a stop deep in the southern pine forest between the towns of Mimico and Middleville. Maxwell and Bob loved the smell of the pines, but Stu thought they were a bit "whiffy." There were no passengers on this run, only cargo and the mail.

Stu hopped off their mail car and headed to the engine to see what had happened. When he returned, he told Maxwell and Bob that one of the trailrods had split in two. They'd be there half the day for repairs. Maxwell, Bob, and Stu had the remaining mail sorted in thirty minutes, and Bob headed to the cot with his romance novel.

"Bob, why do you read romance novels?" Stu asked. "I mean, most of the folks I see reading those are women."

"To try and remember what all the fuss was about."

Stu nodded as if he understood.

"Maxwell," Stu said, "where is Alexey, the train engineer, from? He has an accent, and I have a hard time understanding him. I don't think he likes me."

"He and his mom emigrated from Russia in 1945. If you want to get on his good side, take him a Coke for his mom."

"His mom?"

"Yeah. His mom was a night witch."

"My gosh, a night witch. Are you sure?"

"Yep, Alexey showed me a picture of her from 1944 wearing her Soviet Air Force uniform, her chest plastered with medals. I've talked with her a few times as she occasionally brings Alexey his lunch. You'd never guess the sweet thing was a wicked night witch."

"Wow! They had it rough, didn't they?"

"Sure did. Our guys in Bomber Command had a hard time, but at least they had modern equipment and could return to the US after twenty or twenty-five bombing missions over Germany. But these Soviet women lived close to the front lines, close to their targets—Nazi combat troops—and flew five, ten, or even fifteen bombing runs a night in outdated planes with no instruments. Their planes had open cockpits. Imagine the cold night air during those Russian winters! Incredible women. Night witches were what the German soldiers called them because they'd cut their engines and glide down to drop their bombs, quiet as a witch on a broom, and the name stuck."

"Amazing, just amazing. I can't imagine my mom doing that. But why give her a Coke?"

"She loves Coke."

"I thought the Russians didn't allow Coke into their country."

"They don't, but Marshall Georgy Zhukov, who led Russian forces through Eastern Europe capturing Berlin, discovered

Coke and developed a taste for it. He would have his adjutant take some to the closest Night Witch Group as he knew that they had a tough job. So Alexey's mom developed a taste for it too. The Russians still won't let Coke into the country, but Marshall Zhukov wanted some, so President Truman asked Coke to oblige. Now they send Marshall Zhukov his Coke—secretly—in bottles that don't say Coke and with no coloring, but it tastes like regular Coke."

"Gosh! The things we don't know. I think I'll go back to the engine and watch the repairs. I'll take a Coke with me—for Alexey's mom. Bob's still reading, but do you want to come and watch too?"

"No, thanks. I need to write a letter," Maxwell replied. He started typing on the typewriter.

To Whom It May Concern:

I know what you and the sheriff's wife did on Thursday night, July 9. I watched y'all. I heard sounds and peeked. Just because you're pliant, a swinger, and good with your fingers—yes I saw—doesn't mean you can take advantage of women. You think you're cute; but you're just a clown. If you noticed in the paper several months back, Bryant Jackson was sentenced to four years in prison for the same crime. You must stop doing this with the sheriff's wife and make things right.
If you don't, I will turn you in.

—Your conscience

Maxwell had finished the letter when Stu returned.
"You done with your letter?" Stu asked.
"Yep, only need to put it in an envelope," Maxwell said as

he wrote the address on the envelope. Then he put the letter in the envelope and dropped it into the correct mail bin. "Did you enjoy watching them fix the engine?"

"Yes, I did. One day I'm going to apply for a train engineer's position, my dream job."

"One day? Why not now?"

"Well, because of my family, my mom mostly. She believes working on trains is dangerous."

"But you do work on trains."

"My family doesn't know that. I told them I work for the post office, which I do."

"Surely they know something is odd, what with our schedule of six days on, eight days off."

"Not if you work for the post office in Atlanta on special assignments with odd hours, which is what I might have told them."

"Might have." Maxwell chuckled as he patted Stu on the shoulder. "I do hope you can get your dream job one day."

Maxwell sat down at the typewriter and started another letter. After his last visit with Phaedra, he knew it was time to pop the question.

Dearest Delightful Darling,

This is the boldest letter I have ever written. I hope you're ready for it. After what you said the last time we were together, I realize it is time to . . .

. . . I will meet you at the train depot Thursday at 6:00 p.m. If your answer is yes, be holding a red rose when you come to meet me.

Yours Forever,
Maxwell

THE LETTERS FROM THE TRAIN

Maxwell addressed an envelope. Eight hours later when his shift ended, he placed the envelope in the correct mail bin. Then he got off the train to get a few hours of sleep before his next train, the 449 from Tennille.

Phaedra had been watching and waiting for the mail carrier. She sat on the front porch shielded from the morning sun—the porch where Maxwell had made love to her again and again during the past year—eagerly anticipating his letter. Of course, the term *making love* described courting, which was often completely devoid of touching.

As the mail carrier approached the mailbox, he dropped the stack of letters he had been sorting. With all the rain the night before, the letters got wet. Phaedra closed her eyes and shook her head. He took an inordinate amount of time re-sorting the letters after he gathered them from the street. To Phaedra it seemed to take him more time to re-sort the letters than it had taken him to reach their house, one block from the post office, two blocks from the bank, and three blocks from the train depot. Finally the mail carrier opened the mailbox at 213 Maple Street, the home of Mr. and Mrs. Avery Smith and their two daughters—Phaedra, age twenty, and Serenity, age seventeen—and deposited the envelope.

Phaedra waited until the mail carrier turned the corner. Then, grinning, she skipped like a child to the mailbox. The mailbox held one envelope. She took it and went inside. With the envelope in her hand swinging by her side, she could tell it was postal stock. Finally, a letter from Maxwell. Standing in the entryway next to the table that held her father's open briefcase, she tore open the envelope without the slightest hesitation. She laid the envelope in her father's open briefcase and unfolded the letter.

"Yikes!"

Startled by her mother's cry and the sound of shattering china, Phaedra dropped the letter into the briefcase and ran to the kitchen. Her father had bobbled and then dropped his coffee cup as he was rushing to leave for work.

"Sorry," Mr. Smith said. "Phaedra, will you clean this up for me? I don't want to be late."

"Sure, Daddy."

Mr. Smith went to the entryway, closed his briefcase, and headed to his job at the bank.

After cleaning up the spill, Phaedra returned to the entryway to discover that the letter was gone. After a few minutes of searching, she realized it must have fallen into her father's briefcase. She wasn't concerned, as the entire family was considerate of each other's privacy. She knew her father wouldn't read the letter.

When Mr. Smith arrived at the bank, he went to his office on the second floor, put the briefcase on his desk, and opened the window. It was a breezy day, and the bank's air conditioner was being repaired. He went back to his desk and opened his briefcase. He noticed both the letter and the envelope. He picked up the envelope. It had no return address, and the writing was smeared, but he could just make out the name and the street address. The phone rang and he put down the envelope.

"Yes?"

"Mr. Smith, the directors have requested your presence in the boardroom."

"On my way."

When Mr. Smith opened his office door, a gust of wind from across the hall sailed past him, cast the envelope into the trash, and dispatched the letter out the window to the world beyond. Mr. Smith didn't notice.

Later that day Phaedra waited on the porch for her father to return from work. When she saw him approaching, she ran to the sidewalk.

"Daddy, I think I left a letter in your briefcase this morning."

"A letter and an envelope were in my briefcase, but the envelope wasn't addressed to you."

"What?"

"Did you look at the name and address on the envelope, Phaedra?"

"Well, no. I thought it was from—"

"Maxwell?"

"Yes."

"The name on the envelope was smeared, and I could barely make it out. It was addressed to Mr. Roddy Chumble at 213 Mapletree Street. Why the city named one street Maple and the other Mapletree when they're only a block apart perplexes me. Anyway, Mr. Chumble is that professional clown who lives one block over and worked for the circus for many years. He grew up here. Remember he performed at Cindy's birthday party next door. He could swing, climb, and do Houdini-like stunts. It's not the first time we've gotten his mail in error."

"Are you sure? Can I see it?"

"I'm afraid I left it on my desk, and the wind must have blown it out the window."

Phaedra appeared dejected.

"Don't look so sad, sweetie. Maybe your letter will come tomorrow."

"Yes, it will."

As fate would have it, the letter floated down from Mr. Smith's office, gracefully swinging to-and-fro, landing in the empty passenger seat of Mr. Roddy Chumble's Cadillac convertible that was stopped at the red light by the bank. Roddy saw the letter float down to the seat but not whence it came. He pushed it under the carton of cigarettes on the passenger seat. Ten minutes later, when Roddy pulled into his driveway, he grabbed the letter and read. He sat there for thirty minutes, considering his best course of action. He did remember seeing the headline in the paper about Bryant Jackson going to prison.

Although it was dangerous, Roddy called the sheriff's wife, and they arranged an assignation at a secluded spot outside of town. When they met, he shared the letter with her.

"Where did you get this?" she asked.

"Someone from the bank tossed it into my car as I drove by. I didn't see who," Roddy replied.

"My God! Someone at the bank knows about us—about this?"

They agreed never to see each other again. It was not a difficult decision, contrary to what one might think. They had known each other well in high school when they both were incorrigible and sowing their wild oats. After high school, Roddy joined the circus and traveled constantly. He had recently moved back to town while he took some time off. The pair ran into each other last June. Overcome with the excitement of the old days, they decided on a whim to meet clandestinely on July 9.

Their second decision regarding the letter was more difficult, as—truth be told—they both had been dreaming about the upshot of the affair. Finally, after reviewing all the ramifications, they agreed on a course of action.

Phaedra was subdued that evening at the Smiths' dinner table, not eating but moving the food around on her plate. She was preoccupied, thinking of Maxwell. If she didn't get a letter, she would have to ask him straight-out. Her mind was in a tizzy at the thought of being so bold. Tomorrow, she convinced herself, the letter would come.

"I know who's getting married," Mr. Smith said.

"Daddy," Phaedra loudly said.

"Avery!" said Mrs. Smith just as passionately. She had told him to refrain from bringing up the possible future marriage of their daughter to Maxwell, bearing in mind her intuition on the matter.

"What? Missy Count is going to marry Abel Duckworth. I heard it at the bank today."

Avery turned to Mrs. Smith, who looked at him somewhat sternly, and asked, "What, what did I do?"

"We'll discuss it later, dear."

"Excuse me. I'm not hungry. I'm going to my room," said Phaedra, leaving the table.

"Serenity, will you at least stay and finish supper with your mother and me?"

"Of course, Daddy."

The next day she woke up, got dressed, and went out to the mailbox. There was a letter to her from Maxwell. She went upstairs to her bedroom, looked at her name on the envelope again to be sure, tore it open, and started reading. Her pulse quickened. She felt her heart beating in her chest. Fortunately, today was Thursday. She thought about what to wear and when to go to the flower shop.

———∞———

That afternoon Maxwell got to the bank at 3:42 p.m., eighteen minutes before closing, for his meeting with Mr. Smith. Maxwell knocked on Mr. Smith's door which was open.

"Maxwell, come in. Let me wrap up this paperwork before we get started."

"Okay. I do appreciate the time you've spent with me over the past months tutoring me on financial matters."

"I've enjoyed it, Maxwell. Young people—well, most people—haven't a clue how to plan for their financial future. And now I get to teach financial lessons once a month in the bank's conference room because Mr. Rathport, the bank president, became aware of what we were doing those nights in the bank."

"That's great."

"Yes, it is. How was this past week's mail run?"

"We did have a little excitement. The train broke down for a few hours, which rarely happens."

"I am still amazed that with all the mail traveling around this country, the post office does such a good job with so few mistakes, except when it rains."

"When it rains?"

"Yes, yesterday a letter was delivered to our house in error. Part of the address was smeared because it had gotten wet.

Phaedra thought it was from you. She hadn't bothered to look at the name and address before she opened it, but it was addressed to Roddy Chumble."

Maxwell's eyes widened. An intense feeling of something gone horribly wrong gripped his mind and chest. Maxwell dropped down to the sofa, his thoughts traveling a mile a minute. At least he hadn't signed the letter. If he had, would he be considered an accomplice, after a fashion? But now, the law would know about her. He had failed to keep her out of prison.

Still filling out papers on his desk, Mr. Smith didn't notice that Maxwell had sat down.

"But at least no one read the letter. Good thing too; we'd be breaking the law if we had. You know, opening other people's mail," Mr. Smith said as he looked up. "Maxwell, you okay? You're as white as a ghost."

"I feel a bit lightheaded."

"Stay there. I'll get you a Coke. Be right back."

Maxwell's thoughts were flying about. How could no one have read the letter? Maybe the letter had been read and Mr. Smith didn't know. Was an investigation already in progress?

Mr. Smith walked back into the office.

"Finally, it was my turn to go down to the basement and get you a Coke after all the times you did it for me during our nightly tutoring sessions."

"Thanks. How is it that no one's read the letter?"

"Phaedra inadvertently dropped the envelope and letter in my briefcase before she read it. I hadn't noticed it in the briefcase and brought it here. I had a chance to look at the envelope but not the letter before I was called into a meeting. When I got back, the letter and envelope were gone."

"Gone?"

"Yes. My guess is that they blew out my open window, but

I don't know for sure."

Maxwell's mind was reeling. The letter could be sitting on the ground somewhere. It might have been destroyed or could be lost forever. Or it could be discovered in a week, a month, a year, or longer. He had inadvertently left the sword of Damocles hanging over the sheriff's wife, which would be a never-ending nightmare.

"Mr. Smith, can I lie down on the sofa for a few minutes?"

"Of course. I can get started on tomorrow's paperwork."

At 4:55 p.m. Maxwell sat up, wondering what he should do.

The phone rang.

"Yes?"

"Mr. Smith, Mr. Rathport would like to see you in the vault."

"Certainly."

"Maxwell, you've wanted to see inside the vault; here's your chance—follow me."

They walked into the vault.

"Hi, Maxwell," said Mr. Rathport. "I didn't know you were here. How's the family?"

"Fine. Thanks for asking. Do I need to leave?"

"No, Maxwell. You can stay. Avery, take a look at this."

Avery walked over to a table that had a suitcase on it.

"What's this?"

"Open it."

Avery opened the suitcase. "What in the world?"

"A man left it in the bank today. We don't know who. Three tellers have given us three very different descriptions. A note is included stating, 'We're Sorry,' but what's interesting is that it's the money from the robbery we had the night of July 9. All of it."

Maxwell passed out. Fortunately, Daren, the security guard, caught him mid-fall.

When Maxwell came to a few minutes later, he found himself on the sofa in Mr. Smith's office.

"I guess those train runs can wear you down after six days. You feeling better?" asked Mr. Smith.

"Yes, thanks. I guess I needed more than a Coke. What time is it?"

"Five thirty."

"Can I rest a few more minutes?"

"Of course."

"What's going to happen with the bank robbery investigation now?"

"I'm sure the sheriff will drop it. And Mr. Rathport said he wouldn't be interested in pressing charges since all the money was returned. It's funny, but the sheriff first thought it might be Bryant Jackson because he's so nimble with his fingers, but he was already serving time for bank robbery. It certainly was a bit scary realizing that the bank had been robbed when we were here studying."

"Scary in more ways than one. I have another appointment in a few minutes, but first I need to tell you something."

"Certainly."

Maxwell told Mr. Smith about the letter he had written to his daughter.

"Maxwell, welcome to the family. It's a bit of a surprise to me, but Mrs. Smith knew this would happen all along."

"She did! But we don't know if she'll say yes."

"That's true. But if Mrs. Smith is any judge, I'm confident a young lady with a red rose will be at the station at six."

Maxwell had been sitting on a bench for ten minutes, preoccupied with desultory thoughts: Why did Roddy return the money if the letter floated out of Mr. Smith's window? Would she say yes? Would the sheriff's wife be safe now? How did Mrs. Smith know? Would things work out with the Smith family, considering? His gaze focused on the ground as he thought.

A young woman with a red rose walked up to the bench where Maxwell was sitting.

"Hello, Maxwell . . . Sweetheart."

Maxwell looked up, saw the rose, and said, "Hello, Serenity . . . Darling."

The End

5
The Poem and Plagiarism

So live, that when thy summons comes to join
The innumerable caravan, which moves
To that mysterious realm, where each shall take
His chamber in the silent halls of death,
Thou go not, like the quarry-slave at night,
Scourged to his dungeon, but, sustained and soothed
By an unfaltering trust, approach thy grave,
Like one who wraps the drapery of his couch
About him, and lies down to pleasant dreams.

After the readings by the high school students, I spoke to the teacher, "Your students certainly picked some good poems to read."

"They weren't picked, Mr. Morris—they are all original works by the students. Pretty good stuff if you ask me," replied Mrs. Dawson.

"I see . . . some outstanding ones, forsooth."

She gave me a double take, smiled slightly, and walked away. Maybe she thought I meant *forsooth* in derision—*oh really*, rather than *indeed*. Surely an English teacher would be familiar with the ending of "Thanatopsis," arguably the most famous poem written by an American. I knew it because my grandfather had quoted it at the end of his high school valedictorian address in 1923. I had a copy of his speech, and the poem was in the only book of poetry I owned.

As a reporter I loathe plagiarism. I worked at a newspaper in Baltimore for two years after graduating from the Henry W. Grady School of Journalism at the University of Georgia in 1946. A colleague at the paper was caught plagiarizing, and the higher-ups used it as an excuse to fire reporters for trivial reasons. The environment became toxic; employees left like pirates abandoning a ship led by an autocratic captain. Oddly enough, most pirate ships were democratic associations. I left too and moved to Cincinnati.

I didn't have a child in the English class, only a nephew, so it wasn't any of my business, was it? And who would I tell? Her teacher, her parents, the principal? Maybe Perdita herself, so she could come clean? Or—and this idea was brilliant—I could give her mother a book of poems that included "Thanatopsis" and let her *discover* her daughter's plagiarism and address the matter.

But for gosh sakes, it's only high school. I had noticed that Perdita's mother, Mrs. Paisley according to her name tag, was striking with straight red hair in a bob that curled slightly inward at her chin. The makeup around her eyes was understated yet alluring. And since most women sported curls and long hair these days, she stood out. Sometime during the readings, Mrs. Paisley and I glanced at each other, and our eyes locked. It was at that instant I realized she was the former Nova Taylor. I knew her. Well, *knew* is an inapposite description for a chance meeting that had lasted less than a minute on the final day of summer camp about twenty years earlier.

We had literally walked into each other at the infirmary.

I had been holding a cup full of water, and neither of us was watching where we were going. Nova ended up on top of me on a cot. With my legs dangling off opposite sides, I couldn't find the leverage to get up. Her hands were all over me as she scrambled to push herself up. Once we were up, I noticed that my water had spilled all over the front of her T-shirt. I grabbed a hand towel from the cot to wipe off the water. As I wiped her chest, I realized what I was doing and dropped the towel. When Nova reached down to pick it up, she slipped on the wet floor. As she reached out to keep from falling, she grabbed the first thing she could—my belt—and pulled me down on top of her as we fell onto the cot again.

Once we were finally up, I said, "I'm sorry."

"Your name's Tony, isn't it?" she said softly with a slight hint of a smile.

"Yes."

"I'm Nova Taylor." She held out her hand to shake, which I did. "If you wanted to meet me, you could have just said hello and saved your blood a trip to your face."

Yes, I was blushing.

"Have you ever kissed a girl?"

"Kissed a . . . why would—"

At that, Nova stepped forward, gave me a quick kiss on the mouth, and left. I fell onto the cot for a third time. I was in love.

At home the following week, using the phone book and making a series of phone calls that mostly ended with me hanging up quickly, I discovered that Nova lived one town over, but I never saw her again—until the poetry reading.

The next day, Tuesday, I drove to work in my brand-new 1956 purple Cadillac convertible. It was a pleasant spring day, and I anticipated an enjoyable morning drive since I lived ten miles out of town. My friend Charlie, my deceased father's best friend, had bought the same car several months ago. Although Charlie had to replace one of its four mufflers every six weeks or so, I loved the car and the color and wanted one. As the wind disheveled my hair, a pleasant sensation, I thought about "Thanatopsis," Perdita, and Nova. And I just couldn't attenuate my aversion to Perdita's plagiarism.

Suddenly I heard a police siren behind me and pulled over. I realized I had been distracted and was driving about ten miles over the limit. A deputy walked up to the side of my car.

"Yes sir, deputy . . . oh . . . I mean, ma'am . . . uh . . . sorry. I wasn't aware we had any female deputies in the county."

"You and everyone else it seems."

"Was I speeding? It's a new car, and it's easy to forget that the speed limit drops once you're within two miles of the city limits."

"Yeah, don't know why it drops like that. Maybe a leftover speed trap from the old days. You were going twelve miles over the limit. If it were under ten, I could give you a warning, but I'm afraid twelve miles over is going to bump you up to a ticket and a fine, Mr. . . . ."

"Mills, Tony Mills. Twelve miles over, you sure?"

"Yes, sir. I was pacing you."

"Pacing, what's that?"

"I follow you, then look at my speedometer."

With the sun in my eyes, her sunglasses, the deputy's uniform, and her hair pushed up under her hat, I couldn't be sure that she was Nova Paisley, so I glanced at her chest. I always feel awkward right-out looking at a woman's chest, not knowing if she'll feel aggrieved. But—as with most things—it's context. Yep, she was Nova Paisley. Her name tag read Deputy Sheriff Paisley.

"Have we met? You look familiar," I said innocently.

She raised her eyebrows and said skeptically, "You and everyone else trying to get out of a ticket."

"No, really. You're Mrs. Paisley, Nova Paisley. I saw you last night at the poetry reading. Your daughter Perdita was one of the students who read."

Deputy Paisley stopped writing the ticket and regarded me, her eyes as lovely as the night before.

"Oh, you were there? You have a child in that class too?"

"Me? Oh no. I'm not married. I was there for my nephew. My brother and sister-in-law had some issue with the chimpanzees they're training to be peasants and asked me to go in their place."

"You mean presents?"

"No, peasants. Apparently Joseph McCarthy's brother-in-law has an act that makes the rounds with various circuses. It's some kind of skit about the dangers of communism."

Nova frowned at me questioningly.

"Hey, I know—but I'm just telling you like it is. I don't pay much attention to what they're doing as I want plausible deniability. By the way, I don't recall seeing Mr. Paisley at the reading last night."

"He died in Korea five years ago."

"Oh, I'm so sorry. I didn't mean to—"

"That's quite all right, Mr. Mills."

"Tony, please."

"Not while I'm on duty, Mr. Mills. If you have trouble with your chariot, call me. I understand the mufflers can be a problem on this model, and I'd love to get my hands on your motor."

It's prudent not to make assumptions about what some folks mean.

"You work on cars?"

"On weekends and sometimes at work. My daddy was a mechanic. I helped him all the time. And with my acute hearing, I do the tune-ups on our patrol cars. I live at 324 Milfordfork Road, eight miles out of town if you ever need servicing. Here's my number if you want me."

Maybe Nova wasn't being Delphic. She gave me her deputy card with her number written on the back, and she ripped a page from her ticket book.

"Here's your warning. Just watch the limit."

"Warning? I thought I was getting a ticket—twelve miles over the limit as I recall."

"Let's call it deputy's discretion. Besides, I'm no William West."

"William West—who's that?"

At that, Deputy Paisley tipped her hat. Her red hair flowed around her face as she shook it out, and she started walking back to her patrol car.

I turned and watched as she walked, hat in hand, the breeze tousling her red hair, the Smith and Wesson draped on her hip moving to and fro. And I wondered, *Who is William West?*

Deputy Paisley got into her patrol car and floored it, blowing past me doing sixty, at least.

Over the next few days I asked a dozen people who William West was, but no one knew. I figured someone at the paper would know, but no. Now I would have to get Nova to work on my motor.

On Thursday I called Charlie and asked if he would work on my engine early Saturday morning. Sure, he said. Then I called Nova.

"Nova, this is Tony—Tony Mills."

"Tony . . . oh yes, the warning earlier this week. What can I do for you?"

"Well, I'm having trouble with my motor."

"What kind of trouble?"

"It's not running smoothly and sounds funny."

"What kind of sound?"

"What kind of . . . uh . . . well," my *National Geographic* on the coffee table said Lorelei Cranes on the cover, "like a Lorelei crane with its leg caught in a bear trap."

I heard a slight chuckle. "I can't remember the last time my birdwatching group saw a Lorelei crane."

Uh-oh. "Ah . . . well, maybe it was the sound of a Berkshire crane's mating call."

"No doubt. You definitely need me in either case. I'll see you Saturday. Will noon work?"

"Sure, see you then." I hung up slightly embarrassed.

Early Saturday morning I drove to Charlie's.

"So, what's the problem, Tony?"

"I need the Cadillac to make funny noises, but it needs to be able to run."

"What in tarnation? You loco, Tony?"

"No, I met a woman mechanic I have some unfinished business with, so I need a reason to see her."

Charlie burst out laughing and glanced at the ground while shaking his head. "Well, well, don't that beat all. Gracious, Tony," Charlie said, "surely there's an easier way. But for love and the fact that your daddy and I were in the war together, I'll do it. I can change the calibration on a couple of the spark plugs, which will cause it to ride rough. Will that do?"

"Perfect."

"So, what's her name?"

"I haven't named her yet."

"Not the car, you knucklehead—the mechanic."

"You wouldn't know her."

Charlie gave me a wide grin. "Don't want me to know, eh? You must not hold me in high regard. I'll remember that. By the way, there's only one woman in this county who works on cars," he said, chuckling.

As Charlie worked on the car, I thought about the present I had for Nova. It took me a while to find the book of poems I had bought many years ago that included "Thanatopsis." But there could be unpleasant repercussions if she read the book; she could think I was just a cad. Then again, she might never read it, so was there even a point in giving it to her? I thought there was; I thought she'd want to know.

I pulled into 324 Milfordfork Road at noon. Nova was standing in front of a small, enclosed workshop and waved me over to park in front of it.

"Good afternoon, Tony. I could hear your engine a duck's walk up the road."

Duck's walk?

"Sounds as if a couple of your spark plugs need to be re-gapped. I'll take a listen."

Nova walked to the front of the Caddie, opened the hood, and asked me to start her up.

"You can turn her off now. Yep, a couple of your spark plugs are off a smidgen."

"Wow, you could tell that just by listening? You are good."

"That's just the diagnosis. Maybe you should wait until I've got my hands on your motor before you think I'm good."

Uh-huh.

Nova proceeded to pull off some cables, undoing the spark plugs. She took out two.

"How many spark plugs are in it?"

"Eight."

"Eight. How come you're only taking out two?"

"By the sound I can tell these two are causing your problem."

"Goodness gracious, you're amazing."

She looked at me with raised eyebrows. I sat on a stool next to the workbench and watched Nova work. In less than fifteen minutes, she had the sparkplugs gapped and back in the Cadillac. It purred.

"There you go, all fixed up."

"What do I owe you?"

"Nothing, first servicing is on the house."

"First."

"Sure, you're welcome to come back for more."

"Speaking of more, how about dinner tonight at Val's in Montpelier?"

"A bit zippy, aren't we?"

"I do drive a Cadillac. And you're no slouch yourself, what with your patrol car blowing past a man at sixty and leaving a trail of breadcrumbs—or at least one breadcrumb."

Nova stopped putting her tools away and looked at me with the faintest of smiles. "Oh, I see. You want more—"

"Absolutely."

"—information. Pick me up at four."

Information wasn't what I was thinking about at that moment, but I did want that too—Who was William West? "It's a date. Can I use your—"

"Go in the front; it's the first door down the hall on the left."

"Thanks."

I wore a light jacket with the book of poetry in my inside pocket. After I used the facilities, I went to the living room, deciding where to leave the book. I was about to set it down when I heard a voice.

"What's that?"

I turned around and saw Perdita.

"Oh, hi. I'm Tony Mills. It's a thank-you to your mom for fixing my car."

"Can I see it?"

"Certainly."

I handed the book to Perdita. She opened it to the table of contents. After a few moments, she looked up at me. I assumed it was because she saw "Thanatopsis."

"I'll give it to her. She might miss it if you put it on that table."

I hesitated. I couldn't replace the book. What if she didn't give it to Nova?

"Okay." I acquiesced seeing no way out.

I thanked Nova again and headed home. I decided to stop by Charlie's on the way. He was working on his cars as usual.

"Charlie, thanks for the spark plug work this morning."

"Nova got you all fixed up, did she?"

"You knew who she was?"

"Of course. I told you, only one woman mechanic in the county. Besides, she's my second cousin once removed."

"Second cousin once removed?"

"My grandfather's sister's great-granddaughter. Of course, second cousin once removed can also refer to your great-grandfather's sister's granddaughter."

"Why didn't you tell me?"

"You were being a bit ornery with me."

"Sorry."

"Y'all are something else; I tell you that," Charlie said as he chuckled to himself while shaking his head. Then he continued, "You haven't been dreaming about her by chance, have you?"

"Dreaming, about Nova? No, why? That's a weird question," I said with squinted eyes.

"Just a-wond'rin. No reason."

Much later Nova told me that the night of the poetry reading, after she got home, she had called Charlie.

"Hello," Charlie said.

"Charlie, this is Nova. How y'all doing?"

"Fine, darling, just fine. Haven't seen you lately. Things going okay?"

"Yep, just dandy. Listen, the reason I'm calling is I've got a question for you."

"Ask away."

"Tell me, does Tony Mills live at the former Jackson place on the old Adel Highway?"

"Yeah, sure does. Why?"

"I want to give him a ticket."

"A ticket."

"Yeah, a speeding ticket. The speed limit drops close to

town on the old Adel Highway. The trap they used during bootlegging days. I figured I could catch him there."

Charlie burst out laughing.

"My God, girl, if you want to meet the man, go down to the paper and introduce yourself."

"I want our meeting to appear accidental."

"And that's your idea; give him a ticket?"

"Yeah. And I got a hook for him, something I know that he doesn't. It'll keep him coming around. Reporters especially can't let a hook go; they want to know more."

"Ah, you must know him a tad."

"Nope, never met him. I saw him for the first time tonight at Perdita's poetry reading at school. Mrs. Dawson told me his name. But it's weird, Charlie, I've occasionally had dreams about him on and off for years."

"Dreams about Tony?"

"Yeah, I'm in them too. We're just kids . . . but it's him. I don't know why."

"Well, good luck with your speeding-ticket plan. And next time Doris cooks up a smattering of apple pies, I'll bring you one."

"Thanks, Charlie. Talk to you later. Bye."

Later that Saturday afternoon, Nova finished getting ready for her date and sat down to wait until Tony arrived.

"Oh, Mom, Mr. Mills left this for you," Perdita said as she brought the poetry book over and handed it to her mother.

"Oh, how sweet, a book of poems."

Nova was putting the book down when Perdita said, "Look at poem number fifteen on page sixty-four, Mom."

Nova turned to the poem. "Oh."
"Do you think Mr. Mills knows that—"
"I'm sure it's a coincidence, Perdita."
"What if it's not? You think—"
"I'm sure it is, sweetie."
Perdita paused. "I hope you're right."

People were expected to be dressed up to eat at Val's, and I was—suit and tie. I got to Nova's place at four and knocked on the door.

When Nova opened the door, she wore a cocktail dress: emerald green, V- neckline, basic bodice pattern overlapping below her chest, fitted waistline, and medium length. And the way she had applied her eye makeup was superb. A woman can entrance a man with her eyes.

"Nova, you look stunning—absolutely enchanting."

"Why, thank you, sir. You are a true gentleman," she said with a slight curtsy.

She slid her arm around mine, and we walked to the car arm in arm. I had put the top up, figuring she might not want the wind messing with her hair. We got in and I drove.

"You do look grand, Nova."

"Thanks, Tony. This is the first time I've been out since my husband died."

"I'm flattered and glad you said yes. Oh, by the way, we have a friend in common, Charlie. I wasn't aware that Charlie had a second cousin once removed."

Nova giggled. "So that's what I am. I don't see him that often, but when I do, I just call him uncle. You know Charlie?"

"Yeah, he was a friend of my father's when he was alive,

and I've always liked him. I saw him earlier this afternoon. That's when he told me about your relationship. I do have a bit of a confession to make."

"Oh?"

"Yes, I was going to ask you out after the poetry reading Monday night. You weren't wearing a wedding ring, so I was going to take a chance. But after I said my hellos and goodbyes to various folks, you had gone."

"I have a confession to make too."

"Really?"

"Yep. Charlie called me this morning and told me which two spark plugs on your chariot needed to be regapped."

My mouth dropped open, and we both started laughing. She put her left hand on my right hand, patted it a few times, and left it there.

After we finished our meal, we talked for a while. With it still early, no folks were waiting for a table.

"Thanks for the poetry book."

"You're welcome. You read any of it yet?"

"No, haven't even opened the book, but I do appreciate the gesture."

I wondered. Would I be able to get her to open the book? But I moved on to the breadcrumb Nova had left me.

"Are you going to tell me who William West was? I assume he was a straitlaced, ethical person, based on the context in which you used his name."

"Don't tell me an experienced reporter like yourself can't find out who William West was?"

"So far, no. But given enough time, I could."

"How much time do you think it would take?" Nova gave me a quick smile and a flick of her eyebrows.

I smiled back.

"Do you ever plan to tell me?"

"Yes, I'll definitely tell you—sometime. I tell you what, if you'll have supper with Perdita and me next Saturday, I'll tell you then."

"Wonderful."

Monday morning, I phoned the high school.

"Yes, this is Tony Mills of the *Gazette*. The paper would like to do a human-interest story on Mrs. Dawson. I was at the poetry reading last Monday night, and I thought the teacher of that class would make a good story."

"Let me finish writing down your request, and I'll pass it on to the principal. We'll call you back later."

"Thank you very much," I said after giving her my number.

Later that day the principal called me.

"Is this Mr. Mills?"

"Speaking."

"Mr. Mills, this is Doug Morrison, the principal at the high school. I have arranged for your interview."

"Excellent."

"Can you come by the school this Wednesday at four o'clock?"

"I can."

"Good. We'll see you then."

I arrived at the high school a few minutes before four and went to the office.

"Excuse me. I'm Tony Mills. I'm here to—"

"Yes, yes. Go down this hall to the end. Turn right; room number 206 will be the last classroom on the left."

"Thank you."

When I got to the classroom, the door was open. A teacher was sitting at the desk, but it wasn't Mrs. Dawson. I took a few steps into the room.

"Excuse me. I was looking for . . . why Mrs. Tuppence! Gosh, I don't think I've seen you since high school. How are you?"

She stood up, walked over, and gave me a quick hug.

"Tony Mills, it's about time you stopped by to see your favorite high school English teacher."

"I am remiss, no doubt. You look just the same."

"You, being a reporter and lying like that—shame on you."

We both laughed.

After several minutes of reminiscing, I got back to why I was there.

"I think there's been some kind of mix-up. I wanted to interview Mrs. Dawson, the teacher of the poetry reading class last Monday."

"No mix-up, I am that teacher. Mrs. Dawson was substituting for me. She's a math teacher. Based on your message, the principal assumed you wanted to interview me, not Mrs. Dawson. Is that right?"

"Well, yes, it is. But I don't really want to do a story. I want to find out more about the poetry, the readings, and the students."

"Okay, but knowing you, I'm sure there's more to it." She opened a drawer and pulled out a folder. "Here's my folder with the poems by the students. You're welcome to go through it. Is there one in particular you want to see?"

"'Thanatopsis.'"

"Oh, so that's what's got a bee in your bowler."

"Bowler?"

"Bonnet is so overused. I tell you what, flip through each of these poems."

As I flipped through the poems, I saw that they each had the poem's title above the student's name. When I got to "Thanatopsis," under the poem's name was "written by William Cullen Bryant" and below that "read by Perdita Paisley." I looked up at Mrs. Tuppence.

"You were worried about plagiarism, weren't you? You're the person who asked Mrs. Davis about the students' poems. Considering how ethical I know you to be from those high school years, I'm not surprised you found the reading distressing, considering you thought it was the students' own work. Perdita asked me if she could read that poem's ending rather than one of her own. And since she's a direct descendant of William Cullen Bryant, I said yes."

"It's silly, I know. It's only high school."

"No need to feel silly. It's understandable. Especially considering your relationship with Mrs. Paisley."

"Relationship? We've been on one date. And how do you know—"

"I was at Val's Saturday."

"I didn't see you."

"Oh really, and why would that be? Maybe because you two were in your own little world. If there are two people more in love, I've never seen them. But you realize that too, don't you?"

"Yes," I said as I turned a bit red.

"I've felt for a long time that y'all would end up together if you were just in the same place at the same time again."

"Where did that come from?"

"Tony, I was assigned to the infirmary on that last day of summer camp twenty years ago. Even then I realized there was something magical about you two smacking into each other and the kiss she gave you. Something you should know: Nova and Perdita don't like people knowing they are direct descendants of William Cullen Bryant. Almost no one is aware that Nova's first husband only married her for that reason—seeking royalties from a Bryant trust fund. As awful as it is to say, Nova's husband dying in the war was the best thing that could have happened to her. He was a horrible man. Perdita is aware of this and is very protective of her mother and the knowledge of her lineage.

I arrived at Nova's at five o'clock on Saturday. When I walked into the living room, Perdita was there.

"I believe you two have already met," Nova said.

"Hello," I said to Perdita, who nodded.

"Have a seat, Tony. Perdita's about to get supper on the table."

"Okay, thanks," I said as I sat down on the sofa.

Nova sat next to me.

"Nova, please don't keep me in suspense any longer. Who was William West?"

"He is the only police officer who ever arrested a president of the United States."

"You're kidding."

"Nope, the president was traveling too fast down one of the streets in Washington D.C., and William West pulled him over and gave him a warning. The very next day, the same thing happened, except, since the president had already been given a warning, Mr. West arrested him and took him to the police station. The president was good-natured about the whole thing and admitted he was driving recklessly."

"Who was the president?"

"Ulysses S. Grant."

"Wow."

"There's more. William West was a Black man who had been born into slavery. He and the president became buddies after a fashion."

"That's incredible. I have a reporter friend who works in D.C. I'll see if he can find any old articles on the arrest."

"Supper's on the table," Perdita said.

We went into the dining room and were about to sit down when Perdita laid the book of poetry on the table; it was opened to "Thanatopsis."

"Mom says you two are going to be lovers, so I want to know, is this poem the real reason you're here?"

I looked over to Nova, who appeared very calm.

"I've taught Perdita to be independent and think for herself. Although she shouldn't repeat things said to her in confidence. I could be upset with her, but then you already realize we are going to be lovers."

I took a deep breath. There was no way out. I picked up the book, turned to the back of the front cover, and handed it to Perdita.

"That's why I gave your mother *this* book."

As Perdita read, tears started streaming down her cheeks. When she finished reading, she gave the book to Nova, hugged me, and said, "I'm sorry."

Tears streamed down Nova's cheeks too as she read what I had written inside the front cover.

July 23, 1935

My Darling Nova,

You're going to think I'm just a silly twelve-year-old boy, but I Love You. I do believe in destiny and that our running into each other was providence. It had to be: You kissed me. I had never been kissed before. It was more than a kiss. It was enchanting splendor. No matter which ways our lives go, one day we will be together.

Love and kisses forever,
Tony

P.S. I am sorry for spilling the water on your ~~breasts~~ T-shirt and trying to wipe it off. I don't know anything about girls' chests except that they're very personal. I hope I didn't hurt you.

The End

6
You Can't Resign

General Morris Millerant was stunned that Lieutenant Colonel Denton Hammersley had been transferred to the staff of Field Marshall Montgomery as a liaison officer for Eisenhower's headquarters. Colonel Hammersley's prior posting had been with General Patton's Third Army—where General Millerant wanted him—battling Nazis day in and day out in the mud and muck at the head of his troops. General Millerant had pulled ropes several months earlier to transfer the colonel to Patton, a posting that was considered extremely dangerous. Both men were career officers, but their interactions over the years had been minimal. The general was one of those who had achieved his rank through affectation. Now even he didn't know who he was. The colonel wanted to see combat, and the general wanted to oblige. The general's endeavor was not a kindness but an effort to hasten the colonel's demise. The general had seen his wife, Lydia, and the colonel in an embrace seven months prior at the Crown Prince Hotel in Aberdeen and was obsessed with an avidity to punish him.

Crown Prince Hotel – Aberdeen – Seven Months Earlier

Lydia was in her night clothes in room 219 of the Crown Prince Hotel when she said, "Denton, should I tell Morris about us—about you and me?"

"You surprise me, Lydia. You're the one who's wanted to keep this secret all these years."

"I know. I've always felt embarrassed about being a . . . and about our . . . . But with the war on . . . well, I'm feeling different somehow."

"I never thought your telling or not telling was worth arguing about, so I went along with whatever you wanted to do. But with the invasion of Europe about to happen, now is not the time. Morris needs to be focused on defeating the Germans, not the fact that his wife and I are—"

"There will never be a right time, will there?"

"Who knows. It's easier to just leave it alone."

At that they walked to the door holding hands. Denton stepped into the hallway. Lydia pulled him to her, and they embraced in the doorway at the very moment General Millerant was opening the stairwell door.

"I love you," Lydia said.

"I love you too," Denton replied.

Morris stepped back into the stairwell and watched through the door's small window before he turned and went downstairs to the hotel bar.

British Field Marshall Montgomery's Headquarters

When Colonel Hammersley was several yards from the entrance to Monty's headquarters in Paris, he saw two British soldiers push a French woman to the ground, one about to kick her. The woman's dress was long, slightly torn, and soiled now that she was sprawled in the dirt. Her head was shaved, but her expression was dauntless.

"Sergeant!" Colonel Hammersley commanded loudly.

The British soldiers drew to attention quickly and saluted the colonel. Although he had been at the headquarters only ten days, everyone respected him. Even British soldiers admired an esteemed recipient of the United States Medal of Honor.

One of the soldiers piped up and said, "She's only a—"

"I know what she is, Sergeant. I'll be escorting this woman to my office to get cleaned up. Any objections?"

"No sir," they both said.

"What is your name, Miss?" Colonel Hammersley asked as he extended his hand to help her up.

"Marceline La Clair."

"Miss La Clair, come with me, please."

Miss La Clair followed the colonel into the building and was following him down the hallway when the colonel stopped and turned to Miss La Clair.

"Walk with me, please."

"But," said Miss La Clair with a confused expression. "I am walking with you."

"No, Miss La Clair, you're walking behind me, not with me."

Miss La Clair looked into the colonel's eyes and he into hers. The colonel tilted his head down slightly, raised his eyebrows slightly, and gave a quick nod to his right. She took a few steps to stand *next* to the colonel, on his right.

"Is this better?"

"Better."

"Perchance you are concerned that I have a weapon. Is that why you don't want me walking behind you?"

"Despite your hairstyle, I'm confident you're unarmed. You're not the type. But your station in life doesn't mean you should be subservient and walk behind me."

"My station?"

"Female, Miss La Clair, female. And French some might add."

Miss La Clair didn't hesitate and walked *with* the colonel. They were the object of quite a few stares and double takes as they walked down the hall to the colonel's office. Even Monty, whom they passed, knew better than to ask what he was doing with *that* woman.

The colonel stopped in front of Sergeant Randolph's desk.

"Sergeant, I need a large bowl of water and a couple of towels so Miss La Clair can get cleaned up. Bring them to my office straightaway."

"Yes sir," the sergeant said with no distinguishing expression. He knew that second-guessing the colonel was never wise.

Opening the door to his office, the colonel nodded for Miss La Clair to go in. He left the office door open.

"Miss La Clair, please take a seat. Why did you come here?" the colonel asked as he walked over to his desk and sat down.

"I am looking for work. I have taught both English and German, and I can type. I thought I could be useful."

"Miss La Clair, you seem intelligent. You certainly must be aware that with your hairstyle, you wouldn't be given a job here. And exactly why were you given such a style by your French *friends*?"

"A friend of mine was a colonel in the Waffen-SS."

"I see. Were you in love with this colonel?"

"Not in the way you think. He never asked for anything from me other than friendship. We were never lovers. He greatly encouraged me in my studies to become a doctor. It was a joy to spend time with a man who encouraged my intellectual pursuits and allowed me to be my own person with no expectations of favors in return. But you wouldn't understand."

"I don't know; I expect a cousin of Amelia Earhart's would understand."

"You are a cousin of Amelia Earhart?"

"I didn't say that."

"But you . . . you're a funny man."

"Rarely, Miss La Clair," said the colonel with a slight grin.

Sergeant Randolph knocked on the door and brought in a large bowl of water and several towels. "The water's warm, sir."

"Thank you, Sergeant. That will be all."

"Miss La Clair, if you'll excuse me. I'll be back in a few minutes. You might want to wash up."

The colonel stepped out to Sergeant Randolph's desk.

"Sergeant, I'll be back in a few minutes."

"Ah . . . the woman, Miss La Claire, sir. It's okay for her to stay in your office?"

"The desk drawers are locked and the door is open."

"Very good, sir."

When Colonel Hammersley returned, he was carrying a file folder. As he entered his office, he noticed Miss La Clair facing the back wall using a towel to clean off her chest. The upper half of her dress was unzipped and hung around her waist, her bare back facing him. The colonel cleared his throat and walked slowly to his desk while looking through the file folder. Miss La Clair pulled up her dress, zipped it, and returned to the chair in front of the desk.

"Is women's underwear in short supply?" the colonel asked.

"I'm sorry, women's underwear?"

"Bras, are bras in short supply?"

"Yes, they are. The one brassiere factory in northern France went through a changeover. It now makes dog food and manufactures artillery shells for the German 88s."

"Dog food?"

"Yes, apparently Hitler's dogs like French cuisine."

Colonel Hammersley burst out laughing while Miss La Clair donned a grin, her first in many months.

General Millerant's Headquarters
(Phone call with Russian Major General Chekhov)

"Sergeant, get Captain Tanner on the phone," said General Millerant as he walked into his office and closed the door.

"Your call, sir," the sergeant said over the intercom.

"Captain Tanner, this is General Millerant of the Seventh Army."

Instead of the somewhat familiar voice of Captain Tanner, the general heard loud laughter on the other end of the line, then someone speaking English with a Russian accent.

"General Millerant, good to hear from you. This is Major General Ivanovich Chekhov of Russia's Eleventh Army. I didn't realize I had given you my number."

The two generals' families had spent a month together in 1936 as part of a diplomatic effort to foster international understanding.

"General Chekhov, what the devil?" General Millerant said.

"Ah, but at least we both are devils. Tell me, you still headquartered outside Paris?"

"And you, General, outside Brest?"

"Touché. It is best to know where your friends are and your enemies too. Are you calling to request help? Perhaps I can send you some of our spare tanks by way of Berlin since we have so many. I imagine we can meet up at the French-German border and save you Americans any further trouble with Germany."

"General, we are most eager to abet the Russian people. Anent that, we will gladly meet you at the German-Polish border after we take Berlin."

"I see you wish to use archaic words with me. If you will bethink, my wife is a professor of English at Moscow University. I hope Lydia is well."

General Millerant's face turned red thinking of his wife's assignation with the colonel.

"Fine, General. How is your wife's cousin Anna . . ."

"Anna Shchetinina. She is fine. Captaining a ship in the Baltic, I believe."

"She is an imposing woman. First woman in the world to command an oceangoing cargo ship. Quite the character and very stout."

"All Russian women are stout, General. That is why we will rule the world one day. Not like your soft, perfumed bourgeois ladies with their painted toenails."

"Women have to be stout to live in Russia. But western women are intrepid, apt, and perspicacious. And as far as Russia ruling the world, you're hanging noodles on my ears."

General Chekhov cachinnated at the general's use of the Russian proverb for a lie. After the laughter had abated, General Millerant continued.

"General Eisenhower wanted me to call and ask how your latest offense against the Germans is going." Of course, General Millerant was feigning.

"Tell your commander that things are going well. The hapless Germans are shilly-shallying. So much so, that half our troops are on leave while our cleaning ladies are pounding the Germans' noggins with their own brooms," said General Chekhov as he let out more booming laughter.

General Millerant's Headquarters
(Phone call with Captain Weston)

"Captain Weston, General Millerant here," the general said over the phone.

"Yes sir, General."

"I need Colonel Hammersley transferred to my command ASAP."

Captain Weston was the officer in charge of processing transfers.

"I'll need your written request and . . . wait, wasn't he just transferred to Monty's staff from Patton's Third?"

"That's right."

"That'll be hard to do, General. Another transfer so soon will raise red flags."

"My written request is on its way as we speak. It will arrive any minute now. And to help smooth things over, a case of Tennessee's finest is in the jeep, all yours. That's right, Captain, bottles of Jack Daniels."

"Well, I don't know, sir . . ."

"Also, Captain, I understand your girlfriend is French."

"Yes sir."

"Also in the jeep are several brand-new imported silk bras, which your girlfriend may appreciate."

"Wow! Those are in short supply."

"Don't I know it . . . I mean, so I understand."

"I'm typing up the transfer order as we speak. I'll send it through in the morning, sir."

"Pleasure doing business with you, Captain."

General Millerant's Headquarters
(Meeting with Colonel Hammersley)

"General Millerant," the colonel said as he saluted.

"Colonel Hammersley," the general replied as he saluted back. "Have a seat."

"Thank you, sir, but I'll stand."

The general, the colonel, and the general's aide, Major Narmore, were in the general's office, not far from Paris.

"Major Narmore, you're dismissed," General Millerant commanded.

"Yes sir." The major left the office.

"Colonel, how would you feel about being transferred from

Montgomery's staff to lead a mission inside Germany?" General Millerant asked, knowing the answer.

"I always prefer action, sir."

"I'm well aware of that, Colonel. The transfer has already been done. A mission has been planned which, if it succeeds, will end the war. I must warn you that the mission is dangerous, and a high casualty rate is expected. Still interested?"

"Yes."

"The mission is as follows: you and five others will be parachuted into Wiesbaden, Germany."

"Ah, begging your pardon, sir, but a C-47 has almost no chance of making it to Wiesbaden with all the German fighters and antiaircraft guns."

"You'll be flying at night, and the C-47 will be flying close to the ground. You won't be spotted. In Wiesbaden you'll go to the Convent of Mercy. There you will contact five others—nuns, actually—who will join the team. The code phrase to find these nuns is 'Peace be with you' in German."

"Pardon again, sir."

"Yes, Colonel?"

"You're not Catholic, are you?"

"No, I don't see what—"

"'Peace be with you' is a prominent refrain with Catholics, sir. The code phrase might as well be 'Hi.'"

"You're smart, Colonel. You'll figure it out. Besides, we don't have time to smuggle a new code phrase to the nuns. Then your team will don disguises as nuns."

"Sir?"

"Yes, Colonel."

"With the bra shortage, we won't have the equipment to disguise ourselves as nuns."

"We've shipped bras to the nuns."

"From where, General?"

"From where, what, Colonel?"

"Where were the bras shipped from?"

"Why . . . why would that matter?"

"Well, I wouldn't expect the Germans to be letting packages into the country willy-nilly, especially bras. It is well known that the nuns of the Convent of Mercy take a vow of minimalism and don't wear bras. The package was probably flagged by the Gestapo."

The general stared at the colonel. You could almost see the wheels spinning. Perhaps not spinning as much as coming loose. But the general continued outlining the plan.

"You will be provided with a bus. Your team will drive to the Wolf's Lair in western Poland."

"Sir?"

"Yes, what is it, Colonel?" the general said, letting out a long sigh.

"It's at least 800 miles to the Wolf's Lair from Wiesbaden. Due to the gas shortages in Germany, the trip to the Wolf's Lair could take weeks. And that doesn't even consider the state of the roads after months of British and American bombing."

"The nuns have been saving their ration coupons. And you'll be given a map showing which roads are intact. Besides, the nuns raise sheep. As a backup plan, you can always herd the sheep over the rivers and through the woods to the Wolf's Lair. Once you're there, you will kill Hitler and destroy the Wolf's Lair. Afterward, you will meet up with Polish partisans who will whisk your team over to Major General Chekhov of the Russian Army."

"Sir?"

"Yes."

"Based on the advance of the Russian Army, I expect Hitler has left the Wolf's Lair."

"Our intelligence people say he's still there."

"Are these the same intelligence people who mailed the bras, sir?"

"Colonel, like most missions of this kind, much of what you need to do will have to be improvised."

"Ah, one more thing, General."

"What is it now?"

"Our handoff to General Chekhov."

"Yes?"

"I understand that the Germans halted the advance of General Chekhov. It seems that the Germans captured all of the general's cleaning women, and the Russians are bogged down in trash."

"I spoke with General Chekhov not long ago. Their advance is on track."

"And what is the timetable for the mission?"

"The plane is gassing up now. You need to be at the airfield in forty-five minutes."

"This mission has no chance of succeeding. I am sorry, General, but I refuse the assignment."

"Colonel, you have no choice. The assignment has been made. Do the best you can."

"In that case, General, I regret to inform you that I am resigning my commission in the United States Army."

"Colonel, Colonel, *you can't resign*, especially not during a war. And with the new policy on soldiers who go AWOL, you could be shot."

"I can resign, sir. I've got permission. A get-out-of-the-army-free card, if you will."

"I'm pretty sure, Colonel, there is no such thing."

At that, the colonel pulled out a paper from his briefcase, unfolded it, and handed it to General Millerant. The letter read as follows:

To Whom It May Concern:

Lieutenant Colonel Denton Hammersley, if he was to so choose, may resign his commission in the Army of the United States unconditionally and anytime with no advanced notice required.

So ordered by the Commander and
Chief of the United States Armed Forces
Franklin Delano Roosevelt, President

The paper was signed.

"Colonel, you don't expect me to believe this is real, do you?"

"The president and I were friends in school. He likes me."

"Well, you're in luck, Colonel. I happen to have a man on my staff who was assigned to the White House in the past. I'm sure he is familiar with the president's signature."

General Millerant buzzed Major Narmore and asked him to come into the office.

"Yes sir?" said the major.

"What's the name of that enlisted man who worked in the White House for a while?"

"Sergeant Everland, sir."

"Is he available?"

"I believe so. He should be in the communications office."

"Good, find him and report to me immediately."

"Yes sir." The major left to retrieve Sergeant Everland.

Colonel Hammersley sat down, crossed his ankles, and rested his boots on the general's coffee table.

"Get your boots off the table," General Millerant said with a gruff voice.

"Sorry, sir. I'm no longer under your command."

A few minutes later there was a knock at the door, and the major entered with Sergeant Everland.

"Colonel, get ready for the brig unless you change your mind. Sergeant Everland, you worked in the White House, did you not?"

"Yes sir, for two years."

"And you're familiar with the president's signature?"

"Yes sir."

"The colonel here wants me to believe the signature on this letter is the president's. I'm sure it's not, and I need you to confirm that. Do you understand?"

"Yes sir."

General Millerant handed the letter to Sergeant Everland.

The sergeant looked at the colonel, then at the letter, and read it to himself. It appeared that the sergeant may have had to read the letter twice.

Sergeant Everland said, "I don't believe it—"

"See, Colonel, your little fabrication has failed. Major, if you please, escort—"

"Sorry, General, if I may finish," the sergeant said. "I can't believe I used the word *was* when it wasn't true at the time."

"What in God's name are you talking about, Sergeant?" General Millerant asked with a perplexed look.

"I composed this letter, sir; I typed it. I was in the Oval Office when the president signed it and gave it to Colonel Hammersley. But I should have used *were* and not *was* in the sentence. The sentence is a subjunctive sentence, sir. My mistake. I'm sorry."

(Crown Prince Hotel – Aberdeen)

Three days later Mr. Denton Hammersley was having breakfast at the Crown Prince Hotel in Aberdeen with Lydia.

"I can't believe you're out of the army and the war's not even over. But I am so glad."

"The war will be over soon."

"Did you happen to run into my husband while you were in France?"

"I may have; I don't recall. But I do think you should tell him about us."

"Really?"

"Yes."

"But why? I thought you opposed my telling him now."

"I've changed my mind. I think he deserves it."

Lydia looked at Denton, wondering what exactly he meant by *deserves*.

Lydia said, "Well, that won't be an easy conversation. All these years I have lied to him about me, my past, and have not told him about you. I have been ashamed for so long. I know, I know, it's not my fault, but appearances have always mattered in his world."

"The fact that our parents were gypsies who left us on the steps of a convent when we were a week old never bothered me. I've always been glad to have a gypsy as a twin sister. So, go ahead—tell him."

"I'm not sure when I'll get a chance. He might not get any

leave until the war's over."

"Oh, I don't know. I wouldn't be surprised if you see him any day now. Who knows, maybe he's not in the army anymore either."

The End

7
You Still Have to Pay for It

Baltimore, Year 2020

Dan, the bartender, placed a shot glass full of scotch on the counter in front of me. I picked it up and swirled it a tad.

"You still have to pay for it," Dan said as if he hadn't told me that heretofore.

I nodded.

"Your usual too?"

I nodded again as the scotch did laps in my mouth—my mouthwash. A minute later Dan put my usual on the bar, took away the shot glass, and poured the used scotch down the drain. I was performing my bedtime routine before heading to my apartment. I scooped up my usual, ambled over to a booth, and sat down to watch the customers while I drank. I'd make up stories about them, which was cheaper than a movie and more entertaining. Take the priest, the rabbi, and the Peripatetic, for example. I knew he was a Peripatetic because he was always quoting Aristotle and saying the world would be a better place if people followed Aristotle's advice and weren't fanatics. I'd see them two or three times a month.

I used to imagine them syncretizing their beliefs. But two months ago, as I walked past their booth, I heard the priest say to the other two, "Yes, but if the chimpanzee were swinging on the chandelier, it couldn't have been holding the *American Heritage Dictionary, The Complete Works of Shakespeare, The Chicago Manual of Style*, a gun, the purse of the woman who killed her husband, and the mistress's corset." Since then, my imaginings about their conversations had become more contorted and fun.

A woman waltzed into the joint. She stopped for a moment and slowly looked around like she was trying to spot someone on the FBI's Most Wanted list. She slid up to the bar. She glanced over her shoulder at me and then turned to Dan on the other side of the counter.

Dan nodded.

She turned to regard me and headed over.

"Excuse me, are you Gerald Dasher, the private investigator?"

"Yes, but you already know that."

"May I have a seat?"

I nodded. She was well dressed and tidy. Her makeup was subtle and nicely done. Her light-blue eyes could have been enticing if one were interested. She had the bearing of someone who was sagacious. Her face told me that. Or maybe it was an act. Even so, it was a quality I liked in a woman. But I had sworn off women—in the romantic sense—for the time being despite objections from my hormones. I had thought my former girlfriend Brielle and I were on the path to marriage. She seemed to have it all, to be it all. Not long after we started dating, her father hired me—at thirty-two years old—to handle criminal cases at his law firm. Not minor stuff either, but big cases involving mafia guys. And I won my cases. All of them.

YOU STILL HAVE TO PAY FOR IT

The press started calling me Cicero the Younger. Like nitroglycerin, rhetoric, if handled carefully, can knock down castle walls. In high school my English teacher gave me a book of the rhetorical lectures of John Quincy Adams (yes, *that* John Quincy Adams) written when he taught at Harvard, and I was hooked.

After a year of defending mob guys, I started taking more pro bono cases: immigration, restraining orders, free speech, and a few others. Most of these clients couldn't afford a lawyer or at least a lawyer with my pay grade, $750 an hour. I took on so many pro bono cases that Brielle's father ordered me to stop. But I didn't stop, until—

"Gerald, enough with these charity cases. Before you started handling so many, you *had* a great thing going here; at the top of your field, making plenty of money, a great fiancée, and one day maybe running the firm if you'd just acquired a bit more of a liberal attitude toward our clients."

Liberal. He didn't mean it in the sense of *generous* or even *broadminded* but in the sense *of morally unrestrained.* As for *fiancée,* I had thought I would marry Brielle one day, but I hadn't asked her. But like most things with her dad, he didn't ask; he commanded. He would have made a great Gestapo officer, if you could call someone who was Gestapo "great." But he was born too late. Pity. And yes, I did notice he said *had.*

"I am doing pro bono cases. I pick them; I pick all my cases from now on."

"You don't understand; it's over. I don't tell people twice. You've got one hour to get your things and get out." He turned and left my office.

I hadn't lost everything. I still had my skills and Brielle.

Not thirty minutes later, as I was cleaning out my desk,

Brielle walked into the office and threw her key to my apartment on the desk.

"Now I'm glad you never rang my bell. You and your outdated sense of morality; women are just as entitled as men. You're pathetic."

Entitled—She wasn't thinking in terms of *just or proper or equal;* she was trying to justify what *she* wanted. I thought I knew Brielle—that she would understand—but I hadn't realized until that moment that her feigning was Oscar-worthy. I was taken aback. I picked up the key and put it in my briefcase. As I walked out, I stopped next to her and said, "Just because you can doesn't mean you should. What is desired of a man is—"

Brielle slapped me.

"—his kindness."

By then everyone was watching the display. I walked to the elevator. As I waited, the bust of Cicero from my office flew past my ear, denting the elevator door. The elevator doors opened; I stepped in and pushed the G (Going) button. I could have found a job at a dozen other firms doing the same thing, but I wouldn't. So I decided to try private investigating.

"And you are?" I asked the woman.

"Lysandra Woolrich."

Dan came over and said, "Can I get you anything, Ms.?"

Ms. Woolrich looked down at my glass and said, "I'll have what Mr. Dasher is having."

"Oh, thanks a bunch," Dan said as he went to get her drink.

In what seemed like only seconds, Dan came back with Ms. Woolrich's drink and pretty much slammed it on the table. Both Ms. Woolrich and I looked up at him. I knew why he was angry; she didn't . . . not yet.

She took a sip from her glass, flinched, and said, "Ugh, that's water."

"Very cold iced water, Ms. Woolrich. My usual. It's free; Dan doesn't charge for it."

"Iced water?"

"Yeah, you know, like iced tea but without the tea. Didn't you check me out?"

She looked at me and tittered, unsure. "I know that you drink scotch and have an odd sense of humor, so don't think you've offended me."

I laughed. "Scotch, I hate the stuff. I use it for mouthwash. I spray it around my baseboards. It'll kill anything. I see why you need a shamus. You're not very good at investigating. I never try to offend people. On the other hand, I like to be entertaining." I took a sip of my usual before asking, "Why did you pick me? I'm new to the business."

"I know. I believe I might even be your first customer. I picked you for two reasons. First, a week or so ago, I dented a patrol car. I used the opportunity to ask the officer for a PI recommendation, and he mentioned you."

Was that a surprise? I don't know. Even though I had been on the other side of the fence, some of the guys in the department knew I had qualms about the business. A couple of the rozzers said they'd send clients my way.

"What was his name?"

"I don't recall."

"And the second reason?"

"You're not a skirt chaser, searching up a girl's dress for her library card and a quick checkout."

I chuckled slightly. "I'm not the only one with a sense of humor . . . but how would you know I'm not a skirt chaser?"

"An acquaintance of mine works at your old law firm, and

she talked about how you treated people. She was there the day you left and heard you quote the Bible, Proverbs I believe, to your fiancée."

"I count him braver who overcomes his desires than him who conquers his enemies; for the hardest victory is over self."

"More Proverbs?"

"Aristotle . . . and Brielle was not my fiancée. What exactly can I do for you, Ms. Woolrich?"

"A friend who lives in the apartment next to mine is missing."

"Did you go to the police?"

"Yes."

"And?"

"After a few days I checked back in with them. They hadn't located her but said that nothing appeared amiss. I did call her mother, and she said it wasn't unusual for May to move often."

"So, you are worried because . . ."

"Well, several times when we left our apartment building at the same time, I noticed a man would follow her. It was always the same man, and he looked like a gunsel."

I laughed.

"I don't see what's so funny, Mr. Dasher."

"You thought he was a gunman?"

"That's what I said."

"No, not really; that's not what you said. In 1929 the editor of *Black Mask* magazine edited out vulgarities from the stories submitted by writers. Dashiell Hammett was one of the writers, and he liked to try to sneak in a vulgar word now and again to see if the editor would catch it. He figured the editor might misinterpret *that* word. The editor did and left it in *The Maltese Falcon*. Everyone since then has been misinterpreting that word. That's not what it means; it's a vulgar word, or at least it was at the time. But it's hard to tell what's going to offend people nowadays. Even starting a sentence with the word *hopefully* is damnable to some folks. I like to use it as a sentence adverb and ruffle some feathers. Hopefully that makes sense to you."

"What?"

"Never mind."

"What does the word mean?"

"I'll tell you when you're older."

"Older? I'm older than you, forty-two."

"Maybe later. Your neighbor, what's her name?"

"May Flowers."

I raised my eyebrows.

"That is her name. We both moved into our apartments around the same time two months ago. We would hang out together, usually on the weekends, and got to be friends. On several occasions, from a distance, I did notice this nefarious-looking man following her."

"Where did she work?"

"She worked for a temp agency, so somewhere different every week or so."

"Do you know the name of the temp agency?"

"No, sorry. I don't remember."

"Ms. Woolrich, before we go any further, we should discuss fees."

"Certainly."

"I charge a thousand dollars a day plus expenses. I need a retainer of five thousand dollars to get started, which will be applied to your fee and expenses. After five days I'll expect a thousand a day in advance. But I don't bill in blocks of less than a day."

"That sounds fair enough, but I can't pay for more than three weeks."

"It shouldn't take that long."

Ms. Woolrich pulled out her checkbook, wrote out a check for five thousand, and gave it to me.

I looked at the check. "You're from Boston?"

"Yes, I'm an actress in a play that's running here. Normally I work in Boston, but occasionally I get opportunities out of state and rent an apartment while the play is running."

"I imagine there's not a lot of money in acting."

"There isn't. Fortunately, I live with my parents when I'm in Boston. They don't charge me for room and board as long as I save 25 percent of my income. And I usually save much more."

"I see. How much longer does your play run?"

"Day after tomorrow is the last day."

"Considering it's late, Ms. Woolrich—"

"Please, call me Lysandra."

"Okay, Lysandra. I'd like to come by your apartment tomorrow morning at nine. I'll finish getting some information from you then, and we'll go from there."

"Fine, see you in the morning. Oh, do I get charged for today?"

"Not unless you want to."

She smiled and her eyebrows went up.

"Goodnight," I said.

About thirty years earlier—March 18, 1990—Boston

A girl approximately twelve years old was riding her bike to the Oscar Tugo Circle to meet her eighteen-year-old brother.

It was four thirty in the morning, sprinkling and cool. Her parents didn't know; they never knew about these outings. She had sneaked out at her brother's request to do him a favor, which could happen several times a month except during the dead of winter.

"You're late, little sister," Johnny said.

"Two minutes, that's all. And it's dark, cold, and drizzling; you should be glad I came at all."

Johnny gave the girl, who was still on her bicycle, a gentle hug. She hugged him back.

"You know I appreciate it when you help me out, Sis."

"I know. Another of your paintings to take home?"

"Yep. You know how much I enjoy Mrs. Tunney's art class. She says I have real talent. Here's the mailing tube with my latest painting. Finished it last week, so it's dry."

"Johnny, I don't like it when you stay out all night like this, and I'm afraid—"

"Nothing to be afraid of. Just having a little fun with Brian. I'm grateful you take my paintings home for me now and then."

"Put this one in your room?"

"Nah, keep it in your room. I'll get it sometime; no rush."

"All right. I'd better get going."

"Be careful riding home."

"I will."

When she got home, she put the mailing tube in the back of her closet. The following weekend Johnny and Brian disappeared. They were last seen taking a hot air balloon ride. The winds that day could have taken the balloon over the ocean—maybe, or maybe not—but the boys were never seen again. The police had no serious reason to believe that foul play was involved in the boys' disappearance despite both being juvenile delinquents.

Baltimore, Year 2020

I arrived at Lysandra's apartment building a little early, so I could speak with the manager first.

"Mr. Morris, I'm Gerald Dasher. We spoke on the phone," I said as I showed him my PI license.

"Yeah, what can I do for you?"

"I want to ask you about May Flowers."

"Oh, yeah. Ms. Woolrich said she is missing."

"Do you think she's missing?"

"I wouldn't know. Some tenants have a routine, speak to me often, that sort of thing. Them I might know if they were missing. But the ones that keep to themselves, like Ms. Flowers, I wouldn't know. I've got no reason to believe she is or isn't."

"What does she look like?"

"Average height for a woman. Black hair past her shoulders and middle-aged. She wore a big floppy hat and sunglasses the times I talked to her."

"How often did you see her?"

"I'd see her a time or two each week but rarely spoke to her."

"Can I see her application?"

"Sure, but there's not much on it. She paid one year in advance plus the deposit, so I didn't need to get her employment information or past rental history."

Mr. Morris was right. The application only had her name, the apartment address, and a phone number. I wrote down the number.

"One more thing, Mr. Morris. Ms. Woolrich said she saw

a man following Ms. Flowers on several occasions. Did you?"

"Not that I recall."

"Thank you."

"Sure thing. Probably not much help. Oh yeah, one more thing, she always wore a wig."

"How do you know that?"

"My wife. On Mondays she brings me lunch. Ms. Flowers was checking her mail when Florence walked in. Florence, she's a hairdresser, told me later that Ms. Flowers was wearing a wig. I wouldn't have known."

I nodded.

At Lysandra's apartment I knocked on her door. She opened it.

"Good morning. Come in. Sit anywhere."

"Good morning," I said and walked over to the sofa, sat, pulled out my three-by-five notebook and a wooden pencil.

"When did you last see May?"

"Friday morning exactly two weeks ago in the lobby about eight. She was leaving for work, and I was checking my mail. We said hi. That was it."

"What was she wearing?"

"A red-and-white gingham dress, white sweater, high heels, and a white floppy hat. She often wore a hat."

"Describe her."

"There is a picture of her in her apartment."

"I'll see if the manager will let me in."

"I've got a key."

"Oh?"

"She gave me a spare key, and I gave her mine, in case we got locked out or lost the key, something like that."

"Have you been in May's apartment since you last saw her?"

"Yes, the following Monday morning. I hadn't seen her all weekend, and she never answered her phone. I checked again two days ago."

"Did you go through her things?"

"No."

"Last night you mentioned that you called her mother. I need her number."

"Sure." Lysandra wrote it on a piece of paper and handed it to me. She remembered the number without having to look it up. Interesting.

"What else can you tell me? Other friends, where she's from, did she go to college, her dreams for the future?"

"She didn't talk about her past. I assumed she was from somewhere else as I never saw her with anyone. Once she did mention West Broadway Street in Bangor, Maine, but I don't know if that's where she's from."

"You certainly don't seem to know much for someone who purports to be her friend."

"Neither of us are big talkers. We read, played chess, played card games. And when we did talk, it was about what we did in our jobs, classic movies from the thirties, forties, and fifties, music, and politics."

"Did she vote for Biden or Trump?"

"Neither. Said she wouldn't vote for anyone who was over seventy. Said there ought to be a law against it; after all, there is a law about how young a person can be."

"Anything about her hopes for the future?"

"About the future? The only thing she said was that she was going to win the lottery."

"You haven't given me much to go on."

"If I had more, I'd have found her myself."

"Let's go take a look in her apartment."

Lysandra pulled a key ring out of her reticule, and we walked down the hall to May's apartment. Lysandra opened the door and we stepped inside.

"Her picture's over there on the counter," Lysandra said and started walking toward it.

"Stop."

"You don't want my help?"

"Nope."

"What can I do?"

"Just stay there." I put on gloves and took the photo out of the frame. "Not a great picture since she's wearing a coat, floppy hat, and sunglasses. I could walk past her and not know. Why would she have a picture of herself on display?"

Lysandra shrugged.

"Did you know she wore a wig?" I asked.

"What?"

"Did you know that May wore a wig?"

"How would you know that?"

"I'm a detective. Did you know?"

"Uh . . . no."

"You don't seem sure."

"It's not that. I'm trying to recall how I missed it."

I went around the apartment opening drawers and closets, asking Lysandra questions occasionally. She had nothing useful to say, so I decided to finish looking on my own.

"You can go. I'll call you later today or come by the theater this evening. Where are you playing?"

"The Piper over on Fourth and Main."

"Okay. Oh, and I'll take the key."

Lysandra frowned, took the key off the ring, and left.

There wasn't much in the apartment. Some clothes, though not many, and not much else. I decided to look in nooks and crannies. Maybe I'd find something that would help me. I pulled the sheets off the bed. Voila! A business card spilled onto the floor. It was for the Hotel Bordeaux, one of the city's older hotels and well past its prime. I took it and the picture.

June 12, 1990—Boston—Police HQ

"Davis," said the captain, "you got any leads yet on the theft?"

"No, sir."

"It's been almost two months."

"All the major players have alibis, airtight. Jackson thinks it was amateurs."

"Amateurs? That's a harebrained idea. You just can't fence those items. You'd need somebody who specializes, and amateurs wouldn't have a clue who could do that. I want the files on my desk by lunchtime."

"Yes sir."

Baltimore, Year 2020

When I walked into the Hotel Bordeaux, the desk clerk was wearing a Baltimore Ravens sweatshirt and looked like she could have played for the team—a tall, strapping woman with a nice shape. A cigarette was hanging from her mouth by a thread.

"Good morning," I said.

"If you say so," the clerk replied.

I slid my PI license across the counter with a C-note under it.

She glanced at my license, used one of those yellow markers on the bill, and put it in her pocket.

"Throw me a pass. Let's see if we can score a touchdown, hon," she said.

I pulled out the picture of May Flowers and put it on the counter.

"Mary Smith."

I looked at the clerk with raised eyebrows.

"Half the people here are Smiths. Must be having a convention." She had plenty of experience selling information as she kept going. "Room twenty-four, second floor. She's in. Came in thirty minutes ago. Hasn't left."

"How long has she had the room?"

"Four days."

"Four days? You sure?" I said,

The clerk looked back at me with a blank expression.

"Hon, I'm not a virgin in these matters. I mean that figuratively, not literally in the physical sense. If I meant it literally, I'd be lying, figuratively speaking."

She caught me off guard with that one, my mind dizzily trying to follow. Was she flirting?

Before I could respond, she continued.

"I need a man."

"I'm taken."

"You're not wearing a ring."

"They're out of fashion. Besides, my partner is high maintenance; I can't afford one for myself."

She leaned over the counter and looked at my shoes. "But you can afford Allen Edmonds?"

"In my business you need shoes that last more than a week.

Kinda nosey, aren't we?"

"Observant. Your partner, what's her name?"

"Abwehr."

"Abwehr . . . God! I bet you need a dictionary going to dinner parties with her. No wonder she's high maintenance."

"Listen, cutie-pie, I'll be back when I need more raillery, but I've got work to do."

"Whatever you say, hon."

I went upstairs and knocked on the door of room twenty-four.

"Come in."

When I walked in, there was Mary Smith looking like May Flowers and sitting at a table eating her breakfast.

"Pull up a chair. Your breakfast is in the bag," May said, pointing to the Bojangles bag on the table across from her. "Ham, egg, and cheese biscuit. You might want to heat it up first."

"These rooms have microwaves?"

"No, I bought one."

"You can afford a microwave, yet you chose this hotel?"

"I like the ambiance."

"You were expecting me?"

"Of course. Lysandra and I used to play a game called *What Would You Do If*. One weekend I asked her what she would do if I disappeared. She said hire a detective. I could tell she meant it, so I slipped her your business card."

"Lysandra didn't mention that, about the business card."

"Oh, I'm sure she checked you out on her own. Probably thought it would sound weird, you know, getting the name of the PI from the woman who disappeared before she disappeared."

"Why did you give her my card?"

"Because I want to hire you. I need a PI who's also a lawyer and has client-lawyer confidentiality, in the legal sense. I assume you're finished with Lysandra now."

"Almost. Need to tell her I found you, give her your new address, and give her some money back."

"You can't tell her where I am, only that you found me."

"If I leave out that tidbit, she might think I've been sitting in my office all day with my feet propped up reading Raymond Chandler or peeling potatoes and painting my toenails. She could think that I'm trying to stiff her."

"You can't tell her because I am being followed, or at least I was. I don't want to put her in any danger. And that's why I didn't contact you directly. How about this: I write you a note to give Lysandra. I'll explain things up to a point, and she'll recognize my writing."

"That will do."

"Good. Here's the note." She slid it across the table. I guess this was normal in the PI business—being taken by surprise. "Can I hire you now?" she asked.

"Why not. What do you need?" This was just too interesting to leave alone.

"Good. Heat up your biscuit. After we finish eating, you can pull out your notebook and pencil."

After her last bite May started. "I need you to represent me. I want to claim a reward. The reward is $10 million—I hope—and I'll give you 10 percent of whatever amount I do get. If I don't get anything, neither do you."

"Agreed. You *hope* the reward is $10 million?"

"The reward is for thirteen items stolen in a heist. I only have one item, but it is the most valuable item. Today this item alone is worth over $200 million."

"You have *The Concert* by Vermeer . . . stolen from the

Isabella Stewart Gardner Museum, Boston, in 1990?"

She looked at me, startled. "My, my, you are good . . . very good."

"The only $10 million reward being offered today is for the items taken in that heist. And *The Concert* is the most valuable painting in the world that's been stolen and never recovered. Seems to me that the Rembrandt, *The Storm on the Sea of Galilee,* would be the most valuable of the lot, but since there are fewer Vermeers, it's not. Why not go to the police yourself, and keep all the reward?"

"Three reasons. I need someone who will argue for the full $10 million. Someone good with rhetoric. Also, someone is, or at least was before I moved into this hotel, following me. And finally, there may be some legal gray areas that could keep me from collecting the reward."

"The gray areas being?"

"Two that could trip me up. First, you can't have taken part in the heist."

"I don't see how you could have taken part. You would have been, what, ten or so?"

"Or so . . . yes, twelve. I did take part, not knowingly."

"And the second reason?"

"You have to have turned in the stolen property in a timely manner, and I found the painting when I was cleaning out my closet . . . six months ago."

"Where is the painting now?"

May reached under the table and pulled up a mailing tube. She opened it, gently removed a painting, and handed it to me. I unrolled *The Concert*. It was quite a moment, me holding something worth $200 million. Sure, I liked paintings, but a print was fine with me. I rolled it up and handed it to May.

She put it back in the tube.

"Where do you plan on keeping it until we can work out a deal?" I asked.

She told me where; I knew she wasn't lying.

After she had given me all the details concerning her brother Johnny, and her life story, I went back to my office about midafternoon. I called an employment agency and asked them to send over someone the next morning for a secretary/receptionist position. Then I called the Piper to find out what was playing and the starting time. The play was *Aphrodite and the Pythagorean Theorem,* which started at seven. I also made a few discreet calls to Boston and one to Bangor. I was surprised to learn who lived on West Broadway Street in Bangor, but I was sure he wasn't involved. The employment agency called a bit later and said it had someone for me to interview. The person would be over tomorrow morning at nine.

It was almost five o'clock, so I locked up and walked to Henry's Chili Stand and ordered a bowl. When I got to my apartment, I wrote notes about the case (with diagrams) on my six-by-three-foot dry-erase board. Then I got dressed to go to Lysandra's play.

The play was a bit corny but okay for a local play. Lysandra played a scantily clad Aphrodite. After it was over, I went around backstage to see her. The stage manager wasn't going to let me in until I flashed my PI license and told him I was working for her.

She cracked the door when I knocked and let me in. She was wearing a diaphanous maroon robe, nothing underneath. I had planned to tell her what I found, give her May's letter, and give her a partial refund. But since she made no effort to put anything more substantial on—my zipper's not well oiled, and I want to keep it that way—I decided to give her the refund check and leave.

"I'm finished. Here's the refund I owe you. Come by my office tomorrow at one, and I'll go over the details."

"You found her? She's okay?"

"Tomorrow, at one." And I let myself out.

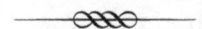

The next morning I went to my office thirty minutes before I normally opened. I unlocked the door to my outer office, wrote "Back Anon" in large letters on the dry-erase board, and left a dictionary on the coffee table. Then I went across the street to a café for breakfast while I read the *Financial Times*. I was going to arrive fifteen minutes late for the interview. I wanted to see whether the person was patient, knew vocabulary, or was at least judicious and brought a book to read. I like people who read.

When I opened the door to my reception room, a book was hiding the woman's face: *Prussian Blue* by Phillip Kerr. She lowered the book, marked the page, and closed it.

"You know *anon* is a contronym?" the woman said. "You could have confused someone."

Prussian Blue, contronym, and her decorum—there was more to her than I had first thought, a lot more, and I knew I would hire her. She was tall, six feet, and wore a bright blue pleated skirt, a bright blue bodice crisscrossing her chest, and bright blue kitten heels on her feet. Her skin was pale white, her lips bright red. Her shoulder-length hair was jet black, and her eye color matched the outfit.

"Good morning, Mr. Dasher. I'm here about a job."

I grinned. "The employment agency sent you?"

"Well, no. The other woman . . . she left."

"You didn't scare her off, did you?"

"No, probably not. Maybe *anon* did."

"Well . . ."

"Ms. . . . Shaw, Brynn Shaw," and she held out her hand.

I reached over and shook. She held her strong and firm grip longer than necessary.

"Well, Ms. Shaw, you certainly look different without your Baltimore Ravens sweatshirt and cigarette."

She smiled. "The cigarette's a prop. I don't smoke. You'd better call me Brynn. And I'll call you Boss."

"You think you've got the job?"

"I know I've got the job."

"Your husband might object."

"I don't have a husband, but I do have a brother."

"Your brother might object."

"My brother is Mike Blackburn."

"I see. I guess he won't."

I didn't know Mike well, but enough. He also worked at the old law firm, but he handled legitimate cases, the only attorney who did. Occasionally we got into conversations on right and wrong, justice and fairness. Our beliefs weren't far apart. Other than that, we had few interactions.

"I like Mike," I said.

"I know. We like you too."

We.

"I always assumed Mike knows things, things he shouldn't. That would explain why he gets to pick his cases."

"And that's why he gets a good raise each year."

"That could be dangerous for him."

"Not a chance. He's got a fail-safe system in place—more than one—and the firm knows it."

"Why were you working at the hotel?"

"I was on assignment. I was working for another PI firm.

Been working for them for about ten years."

"Was?"

"Assignment was done. Figured you could use some help, being new to the business, so I quit," she said as she turned away from my gaze.

In the mirror I could see her blushing. I turned around and walked over to the window.

"I suppose you have references?"

"After a fashion. The PI agency was a bit put out with me, so I have nothing from them. At least not yet. But I have this."

Brynn started unpacking items from her briefcase and scattered them over my desk.

I sat down.

"These are photos of me wrestling in college. We won the state championship. I can handle myself."

I had already figured that. People don't work undercover for a PI firm for ten years if they can't.

"And here's a copy of my diploma and transcripts."

The diploma was for a master's degree in English. "You went to Harvard?"

Brynn nodded.

"Can I ask you a question?" Brynn asked.

"You can since you're working for me."

The corners of her mouth turned up, and I saw a flash of stardust in her eyes.

"Abwehr?" she said.

"It has a beautiful sound to it, don't you think—if you pronounce it correctly? It'd be a wonderful name for a girl or woman."

"The name of German military intelligence from 1920 to 1945 might not be a popular choice. And most people would need a dictionary to pronounce it right. As a matter of fact, I couldn't find Abwehr on any list of names."

"You looked?"

"Of course."

"Some of the higher-ups in the Abwehr worked to thwart Hitler's military plans and were even involved in plots to overthrow him."

"Still, guilt by association in this case is too much to overcome."

"Probably so. Shall we talk about your pay?"

Brynn reached over, put her hand on mine, and said, "Whatever you want to give me, I'll take."

Flirting can be enjoyable, especially if the woman means it.

"Let's get down to business."

I proceeded to tell Brynn about my work for Lysandra Woolrich. Also that Lysandra would be coming to the office at one to wrap up the case. Then I told her about May Flowers, who Brynn knew as Mary Smith. I told her everything I knew about both cases, except for one thing. But I expected she'd figure it out after our meeting with Lysandra.

May 18, 2020, (five months earlier) Woolrich House, Boston

The man had been watching the Woolrich house for several weeks and knew the family's schedule. No one would be home for another three hours. It was two in the afternoon. He walked to the front door, pulled out a key, and went into the house. He looked through the house and finally ended up in Lysandra's room. Finding the mailing tube, the man opened it, pulled out the painting, and looked at it. He rolled it back up and put it in the closet the way it was. He looked through the rest of Lysandra's room and finally went downstairs and sat on the sofa. He thought about whether he should go. There was a flight out of Boston at eight that evening. He could take the flight, leave the country, and go home. He should have, but he didn't. He decided to stay and follow her. He couldn't leave it alone now. Maybe he would have gone home if he had known about the bullet that so badly wanted to meet him.

Baltimore, Year 2020

I was in the inner office while Brynn was seated at the receptionist's desk. Lysandra walked in for her appointment.

"Oh . . . ah, I have an appointment with Gerald at one," Lysandra said to Brynn.

"Certainly; he's expecting you. Follow me."

Brynn walked into my office with Lysandra following. Brynn walked over to the window, pulled herself up on the windowsill, crossed her legs, took out her notebook, and focused her eyes on Lysandra.

"Lysandra, have a seat," I said as I gestured to a chair.

"Who is the . . ." Lysandra said while nodding her head toward Brynn.

"Excuse my manners. This is Brynn Shaw, my secretary. And Brynn, this is Lysandra Woolrich."

"Nice to meet you," Lysandra said.

Brynn nodded and smiled.

"I wasn't aware you had a secretary." Lysandra's gaze lingered for a few moments on Brynn.

"She's new but trustworthy. She is up to speed on your case."

"Of course."

"I did find May, and she prefers that her whereabouts remain secret. She wrote the following note for you."

Lysandra picked up the note, walked over to the filing cabinet, and leaned against it as she read. She appeared to read it several times.

"I see. Is May in any danger?"

"Not that I'm aware of."

"Okay, I guess I'll go home after the play ends. Thank you for your help and putting my mind at ease."

She walked over and shook my hand.

"And good day to you, Ms. Shaw."

Brynn nodded, and Lysandra walked out of my office and then out of the reception area. Brynn walked out to the reception area and locked the door to the hallway. She turned and came back into the office.

"So, what do you think?" I asked Brynn.

"Well, you didn't tell me everything."

"Oh."

"You didn't tell me that Lysandra Woolrich and May Flowers are one and the same."

"What makes you say that?"

"Body language. A person, especially an actress, can change her looks and her voice. However, a person's body language is mostly unconscious. Her body language matches Mary Smith ... excuse me, May Flowers. But what tipped you off?" Brynn asked.

"My pencil."

"Your pencil?"

"Yes, when I met May, she told me to take out my notebook

and pencil. How many people write with a pencil these days? Lysandra knew I did."

"So why is she going through such a rigamarole?"

"I suspect that someone was following her in Boston, and she wanted to use the setup to lose him."

"But that would mean no one was following May; the person was following Lysandra."

"That's my guess."

"Do we tell Lysandra we know she and May are one and the same?"

"I don't know yet."

"So, what's our next step?"

"We'll endeavor to help Lysandra, or May, if you will, collect the reward. But we need to find the guy who's been following her. Why wouldn't this guy have grabbed the painting by now? Unless it's not just about the painting. We don't have the full story; something's missing, which is why we need to find this man."

"How are we going to do that?"

"Good question. Let's roll in the dry-erase board, lay out all the pieces, and see what we can come up with."

We decided that we needed Lysandra to be Lysandra, not May. Then we could follow her and catch the guy.

"Let's take in a play tonight. What do you say?" I asked Brynn.

"I thought you'd never ask."

I sent Brynn on a couple of errands. I needed her to go by my place and pack a suitcase; she needed to run by her place and do the same. There was one more call I needed to make to Boston. Brynn got back about five. At a quarter past six, we headed to the Piper. I brought Amor Towles's *The Lincoln Highway* to read in the lobby. Brynn brought *Prussian Blue*.

At seven o'clock we went in to watch the show. Afterward we went around to the dressing rooms, and I knocked on Lysandra's door.

"Oh . . . it's you?"

"Yep, we've got a couple things to finish up."

"Okay," Lysandra said while reluctantly opening the door. "I thought we were finished." She was wearing the same outfit as the night before. But this time she put on a long terrycloth robe over her maroon wrap.

"Not quite. We know you and May are the same person, and you're probably going bye-bye, leaving May all by her lonesome."

Lysandra took a deep breath and thought for a moment.

"You still going to handle the case, the reward case?"

"Sure, but for you, not May. We need you to stay Lysandra full-time."

"I'm not sure I like that. In fact I know I don't like that. You realize that someone is following *me*, not May."

"Yes, and we need to catch the guy."

"I won't do it."

"Yes, you will."

"Look, I don't care who or why. And the guy's not following May. If I keep pretending to be May for a while, problem solved."

"We don't know why he's following you, what he wants, or what his plan is. And when you're dealing with an item worth $200 million, you simply can't leave loose ends to muck up the works."

"It seems you're deliberately putting me on the spot. Is that ethical?"

"You're the one with the stolen painting, and you want to talk to me about ethics?"

"Can I complain to the bar association or something like that?"

"Or something like that. Do we have a deal?"

She sighed. "Lysandra it is."

We spent thirty minutes in the dressing room going over our setup with Lysandra. After she dressed we followed her back to her apartment. Lysandra said she was not followed all the time, and she had no idea who he was. She never saw him up close or without a hat and sunglasses. We didn't notice anyone following her that night. Brynn and I were going to stay with Lysandra whenever she was home. We brought our suitcases up to her apartment.

I told Lysandra she would have to stay in town until we caught the guy. We followed Lysandra for a few days. Brynn and I switched back and forth following the guy to keep him from noticing. Brynn was a pro at this, and we had no trouble staying clandestine. After a couple of days, we picked out an alley where we could grab the guy. It was a long alley with an alcove midway. We planned it so that when Lysandra left the apartment building, she would walk down the street and turn into the alley. Brynn would be waiting farther down the street in case the guy walked on past the alley. I would be waiting in the alcove of the alley and grab the guy as he walked by me.

We were in Lysandra's apartment going over the plan one last time. We didn't know if the guy was waiting to follow her, but he had most days, so we decided to give it a whirl.

"Okay, we ready?" I asked Brynn and Lysandra.

They both nodded. Brynn left first to get into position down the street. About five minutes later, I headed for the alley. Lysandra left two minutes after me. I went into the alley once I saw Lysandra and the man heading my way.

When Lysandra reached the alley, she turned in. About

twenty seconds after she passed me, the man walked past. I grabbed his arm, swung him around into the wall, and held him with my arm and weight against the bricks. Lysandra had turned back and was standing just behind me. Brynn was coming down the alley by then. I let go of the man who was propped up against the brick wall. His hat and sunglasses had fallen off in the melee.

"You!" Lysandra said.

"Hello, Sis," said the man with a chagrined expression.

Her brother Johnny I surmised. Johnny's mouth fell open and his eyes grew wide. I turned to look at Lysandra. Her arm was rising; it was almost perpendicular to her body. A pink-handled Ruger 38 special was in her shaking hand. Her face was full of rage. I was too far away to reach her, but Brynn wasn't. She pushed Lysandra's arm up just as the gun went off. The bullet probably clipped a hair or two on Johnny's head before it embedded itself in the brick wall. Brynn grabbed the gun and had Lysandra's arm behind her back.

Johnny was clearly surprised by his sister's hostility.

"You after *The Concert*? Is that why you've been following your sister?"

"*The Concert*, no. I've been following her, trying to figure out what she did with the other ten paintings."

A police car crept down the alley with its lights on but no siren. When it stopped, Inspector Garrison stepped out of the vehicle along with a uniformed officer. I knew who the inspector was but had not dealt with him personally. I heard he didn't much care for me. Of course sometimes what you hear secondhand is right, sometimes it's wrong, but usually it's somewhere in between, so it's best to take it with a grain of salt.

Inspector Garrison acknowledged me with a nod and said,

"Dasher." Then he looked at Brynn.

"Well, young lady, a bit early for a fireworks display, isn't it?" the inspector said to Brynn.

"You know me, Inspector. Fireworks is my middle name."

"Sometimes I think it's your first and last name too."

Another patrol car pulled into the alley.

"We'll take these two downtown. Y'all come by headquarters shortly, and we'll see if we can get this sorted out."

I nodded and Brynn said, "Sure."

As Brynn and I walked back to my office, I asked, "You and the inspector seem to be well acquainted."

"I have been working for a PI firm for ten years. He's helped me before. Besides, he's my uncle."

"I've heard he doesn't like me."

The corners of her mouth went up just a tad.

"It's not that. He just thinks no one is good enough for me."

I stopped in my tracks; Brynn kept walking.

I caught up with her. "You called Inspector Garrison? Let him know what we had planned?"

"Yes."

"I don't remember you telling me that."

"Sorry, we were pressed for time."

"And?"

"I've been at this longer than you. In some jobs experience is a prerequisite."

"Is this what it's going to be like working with you?"

"Mayhap."

"I see."

After we got to the office and picked up a few things, we headed to the station.

"Why are we stopping at this office building?" Brynn asked.

"My lawyer's in this building. I need to give him instructions on some papers I want drawn up. It shouldn't be long."

"But you're a lawyer."

"Not this kind of lawyer."

My lawyer needed more information than I thought. When I got back to the car, Brynn had cracked open *Prussian Blue*.

"Sorry, that took longer than I expected."

"No problem."

Once we got to the station, we worked our way up to the inspector's office. His secretary, Eldia Formus, and Brynn were on first-name terms, and Brynn introduced me.

"So . . . this is Gerald Dasher," Eldia said while giving me the once over. "Well, fine . . . just fine. You and Mr. Dasher go on in. The inspector should be back anytime."

Not just anyone was allowed to wait in an inspector's office alone. I knew that the inspector must have trusted Brynn completely. He came in fifteen minutes later; the police had been busy. They had obtained the whole story from both Lysandra and Johnny and were trying to verify it.

"Johnny had indeed given Lysandra the other ten paintings over the course of a week in 1990. She had no idea that they weren't his paintings. After Johnny disappeared, she didn't want to be reminded and didn't look at them for about eight years. When she did, she realized what they were. It took her about seven more years to find someone who could sell them to anonymous collectors, no questions asked. Money wasn't important to her, so she wasn't in a hurry. One painting would be sold every year or so. She set up a trust in the Cayman Islands, where the money was deposited. Over one hundred million, according to her. She had the money from the trust distributed to charities all over the world. So far that information seems to check out."

"Why did she want to turn in the last painting for the

reward instead of selling it like the others?" I asked.

"The go-between died, and she hadn't been able to find anyone else to handle the sale. She thought getting the reward was the safest thing to do. And then Johnny started following her."

"What about Johnny? He clearly wasn't dead." Brynn said.

"Johnny and Brian were in a balloon. It was blown all the way to Newfoundland, then a storm came up. Johnny doesn't know what happened during the storm. He was found a bit banged up, lying in the middle of some aspidistras by a middle-aged couple on their estate. He had no memory of who he was, where he came from, or even how old he was. They didn't know to look for a balloon or another person. He was a resourceful and diligent young man, so the couple adopted Johnny. I've spoken with them, and it seems like he couldn't be a better son. About a year ago Johnny fell off a ladder, broke his collarbone, and hit his head. He started having dreams about his early life, which is how he pieced things together. He didn't want to go back to his old life or even see his parents or sister. He just wanted to find out what happened to the paintings."

"Lysandra can be charged for a variety of things, but what about Johnny?" I asked.

"He's already been released."

"What!" said Brynn.

"The statute of limitation is up. Besides, I got a call from the State Department. Johnny has diplomatic immunity. He's also the adopted son of the Canadian minister of National Defence."

Brynn and I stayed a while longer at the station. It seemed like she was everyone's favorite adopted daughter. On the way back to our office, we stopped at my lawyer's to pick up my papers.

"You need to see your lawyer again?"

"He should have my papers ready. This will be quick."

When we got back to my office, Brynn plopped down on the sofa. I sat down on the sofa too—at the other end.

"What about your fee?" asked Brynn. "Are you going to be able to collect it?"

"You mean a percentage of the reward?"

"Yeah."

"Well, now that Lysandra's not eligible to collect the reward, it seems we are."

"We? But we don't know where the painting is."

"*We* don't; but *I* do."

"What are you talking about? Where is it?"

I pointed to my safe in the corner.

"You . . . you had the painting this whole time; and you didn't tell me?"

"It slipped my mind."

"You." Brynn threw one of the sofa pillows at me. "Are you going to leave it in your safe?"

"An armored-car service will pick it up in thirty minutes and take it to the museum."

"You're giving it back with the reward up in the air?"

"I have already called the museum, and we've already agreed to a five-million-dollar reward."

Brynn threw another pillow at me.

Thirty minutes later the armored car showed up. The driver's and helper's IDs checked out, they knew the password (Abwehr) that I had given to the museum, and Brynn and I said goodbye to *The Concert*.

"It's been an eventful day. I guess I'll head home," Brynn said.

"Fine," I replied. "Let me give you some employment papers to take home and fill out."

"Okay."

"You should have Mike review this set," I said.

"I think I'm smart enough to fill out my own employment papers. Harvard, remember."

"This is a partnership agreement for this PI firm . . . fifty-fifty, you and me."

Brynn stood agape. "What? Why?"

"You're right. You have a lot more experience than I have, and it only seems fair. Moreover, it would be a beneficial arrangement if we were ever to get married."

Brynn jumped off the sofa, ran over to me, dropped onto my lap, kissed me on the cheek, then said, "Oh what the hell!" and kissed me on the lips.

"I think you'd better go home," I said.

"I think I'd better, hon," Brynn replied.

The End

8
Vacationing on Cornouss

Odessa Rosevare and Rusty Belltower were on a vacation of sorts. They were flying in a small plane from the Eleftherios Venizelos International Airport in Athens, Greece, to the small Greek island of Cornouss. The island was in the Aegean Sea not far from the coast of Turkey. They had known each other for less than three days. Their meeting had been happenstance when they shared a table at the Hungry Bear in Baltimore a couple of days prior.

Odessa was looking around for somewhere to sit. At least one person was seated at every table; only one table for two had a seat available for one. Several tables for four had seats available for three, but Odessa thought it would be wasteful to take the second seat at a table for four instead of the second seat at a table for two.

"Excuse me, may I have a seat while I drink my polar bear?" Odessa asked.

As Rusty looked up from his book, their eyes met; there

was an epiphany between them. It was innocuous, mayhap. It was ten seconds or so before Rusty responded; both were oblivious of time.

"Yes . . . please. Have a seat," Rusty responded.

"Have we met before? You seem . . . familiar," Odessa asked.

"No, I would remember you. But we seem—"

"Connected?"

"Yes . . . sit. You do realize we're going to be—"

"Lovers."

"Friends."

Odessa held her polar bear in one hand and a small wallet in the other. She put her wallet in the back pocket of her red shorts, jiggling her hips to get it to succumb to the tight pocket, which it finally did. Rusty was impressed that she stayed upright while jiggling so, as she was wearing red high heels (a new fashion trend—wearing high heels while dressed in casual shorts).

"My name is Odessa—and you are?"

"Rusty."

"Do you come here often? I don't recall taking you in before."

"First time. Usually I'm translating at this time of day, but I'm between jobs."

"Translating?"

"I work or worked as a Turkish translator. But many organizations have stopped working in Turkey."

"How would you like to go to Cornouss with me the day after tomorrow?" Odessa asked.

"It took you long enough to ask," Rusty said, trying to appear witty, seemingly unintimidated by Odessa's boldness. The epiphany had perchance inoculated him against this bold woman.

Odessa smiled sweetly. "Well . . . you are my second choice."

"Oh."

"My friend Janice was going to go with me, but she ran off to Rio with a flamenco dancer."

"You should have had an inkling. Flamenco dancers seem to do that, scrabble through until they end up in Rio. What made you decide on Cornouss?"

"A dart."

"A dart?"

"I put a huge map of the world on my wall and threw a dart at it. It chose Cornouss. That's the same way I pick stocks. I put a list of the thousand largest companies in the US on the wall and throw darts at it. I've beaten the S&P 500 index five years straight."

"I see. I've been picking stocks the same way," said Rusty.

"Is that so?"

"Yes, except I rent monkeys to throw the darts to be sure my picks are truly random."

Odessa and Rusty burst out laughing, both aware of the scenario by Burton Malkiel in his book *A Random Walk Down Wall Street*.

"The trip," said Odessa, "will give us the opportunity to see whether we'll be just good friends or lovers. You're not one of those people who believe a woman has to get married to have sex, are you?"

"I never thought of it quite like that."

"A man wouldn't."

"I'm not interested . . . I mean in sex . . . I mean if I'm not married."

"Shortsighted, aren't you? What if you got married and the sex part didn't work out: She didn't want to. You were lacking. She sounded like a screech owl during. What she liked, you didn't. You probably believe if someone is *the one,* everything will magically work out like that Perry Como song *Seattle,* 'When you find your own true love, you will know it by her smile, by the look in her eye.' Didn't think about that, did you?"

"Well, no," Rusty said as he tried to make sense of where the conversation was going.

"Typical."

"I'll go to Cornouss with you," Rusty said. In certain moods, a person's body shuts down the rational, logical areas of the brain. Scientists don't know why, it just does. The moods that engender the shutdown are rife in some people. Randy knew that Cornouss had the reputation, or canard (he wasn't sure which), of being the Wild West of the Aegean.

The new friends chatted for a few more minutes. They agreed to meet at the airport prior to takeoff. Once, before the meeting at the airport, Rusty wondered, *What the heck have I done?* But he didn't back out. He disliked those kinds of people; people who said they would, then didn't.

As the plane took off for Athens, the two travelers finally had time to catch their breath and converse. Better late than not at all.

"Rusty, I could try guessing your last name, but why don't you just tell me?"

"Belltower," Rusty said.

"That's a coincidence. That's my mother's maiden name, Belltower. Roxie Belltower. She was born in South Bend," said Odessa.

"Good gosh!"

"What?"

"She's my aunt. That would make us—"

"First cousins. Pshaw! That means we can't have sex. First cousins can't marry, cohabitate, or have sexual relations in the state where we live."

"Why would you know that?" Rusty asked. "Besides, you don't seem like much of a rule follower to me."

Ignoring the *why* question, Odessa continued, "I'm not a rule follower, but I'm not willing to break these laws. Not allowing cousins to marry is why the West became educated, industrialized, rich, democratic, and trusting of strangers—good things that improved everyone's life."

"Huh?" said Rusty, perplexed.

"Just read the book *The WEIRDest People in the World* by Joseph Heinrich and you'll understand."

They both quieted down for a while. Rusty was relieved about the sex, mostly. Not knowing his first cousin wasn't surprising. Because of the hurt feelings at his aunt's wedding about thirty years earlier, his father, Sam, and his father's sister, Roxie, both had moved from South Bend. They had refused to speak to each other since. He knew his father had a sister. And he had heard the wedding story, but only once. Odessa was aware of the wedding story too.

Thirty Years Earlier

"Sam," said Roxie, "you can't let your in-laws come to my wedding dressed as clowns. I will not permit it even though they came to yours dressed like that last month. You hear me?"

"But they are clowns and proud of it. And they're very much

opposed to strict rituals that limit possibilities and progress."

"It won't do. You know, more people are afraid of clowns than global warming?"

"If that were true, wouldn't the government be spending more on coulrophobia than on global warming?"

"Since when did the government spend money on the right things?"

"Are we on *Candid Camera?* Where's the camera? Where's Allen Funt?"

Sam's in-laws did come dressed as clowns, which caused the rift.

Of course that's not the story that Odessa heard. What she heard was slightly different from what Rusty had heard.

"Sure, Sam, that's fine if your in-laws want to pay for my wedding cake," Roxie said.

"But there is one condition. They insist on spending at least ten thousand dollars on the cake."

"Ooh! For that much I bet it will be beautiful. I want it to be German chocolate. Okay?"

"Okay."

When the cake was revealed at the reception, it was enormous—a life-sized replica of two clowns. Well, at least from the waist up. From the waist down, perhaps it was a couple on their wedding night. Yes, Sam's in-laws were clowns indeed.

Odessa still thought the trip could be fun. She held no animosity because of the wedding.

Rusty felt the same. After all, he knew the language. Besides, it'd be a nice break before he started looking for another job. Although Cornouss belonged to Greece, most of the residents spoke Turkish because of the island's long history of belonging to one country and then the other.

The jet finally arrived in Athens where the couple boarded a smaller prop plane that seated eight. They were the only two going to Cornouss that day.

"Here's a brochure with some of the attractions. I've already booked one tour. It's of a twelfth-century castle on the island's northeast coast," Odessa said.

Rusty glanced through the brochure.

"Oh, look at this, Odessa. It's a house Aristotle lived in for a short while. I'd like to visit that."

"Okay, we'll see about booking a tour at the hotel."

"I expect we'll have a relaxing time."

When they arrived at the airport, they were surprised by the condition of the terminal. One of the doors leading inside was off its hinges. The windows looked as if they hadn't been cleaned since the fall of the Roman Republic (27 BC officially, but for all intents and purposes, several decades earlier) or perhaps the birth of Aristotle (384 BC). And none of the stalls in the bathrooms were functioning.

Rusty went to the information counter.

"Excuse me, but none of the bathrooms are working."

"You two tourists?" the concierge asked, looking at Rusty and Odessa.

"Yes, from America."

"Oh, the land of big salaries. The plumber hasn't arrived, but he's due . . ." the concierge looked down at his watch, "in three days. But that's glad for you; the plumber is at the hotel fixing their bathrooms."

"Copy that," said Rusty.

"Yes, what can I copy for you?" said the concierge.

"No, 'copy that' is just an expression. It means okay. You

don't get many visitors from New Zealand, do you?"

"New Zealand? I thought you two were Americans."

"We are, but we watch TV shows made in New Zealand, like *The Brokenwood Mysteries*.

The concierge nodded, remembering that he had still not paid his cable bill.

"Let's go on to the hotel," Odessa said.

When they stepped outside, a donkey cart pulled up.

"You need a ride at the hotel?"

"A limo from the hotel should pick us up," replied Odessa.

The cart driver cachinnated. "A limo, on Cornouss? Someone had pulled off your legs."

Exchanging glances, Odessa and Rusty got into the cart. It was only a ten-minute ride to the hotel.

After they arrived and got their keys, Rusty asked about booking a tour.

"Yes," Rusty stated, "we would like to book a tour of Aristotle's house."

"I am sorry, but it is closed for repairs," responded the clerk.

"Oh, I see. How long before the repairs are completed?"

"I don't imagine soon. It's been under repair—supposedly—since 1956."

"The year 1956?"

"Yes."

"What's taking so long? That could be a popular attraction."

"It's owned by the descendants of Plato, and they're in no hurry to promote Aristotle. The locals call the house 347 BC."

Rusty stood there, flabbergasted. "The year that Plato died, and his nephew was promoted to run the Academy, not Aristotle, his brightest student of twenty years?"

"That's right."

"That seems untoward of the descendants."

The clerk, looking a bit confused, simply said, "Yes."

"Considering that all of Plato's works are known, 80 percent of Aristotle's works have been lost, and those we do have went unknown for a thousand years, that seems like sour grapes."

On a slip of paper, the clerk wrote *untoward* and *sour grapes*. He would look them up later in his American English dictionary. He was always looking to improve his language skills. Then he endeavored to explain. "The repairs stopped when a prominent philosophy professor said that everyone should read *The Republic* even though Plato got most everything wrong and that Aristotle has had a greater influence on civilization."

"Come on. I'm tired," Odessa said. "I'm sure we'll find plenty of other things to do." She grabbed Rusty's elbow and pulled him in the direction of their room.

They both were tired from the long journey, and the castle tour was scheduled for the next day.

Rusty woke up about seven o'clock and headed to the bathroom to take a shower.

Odessa popped her head up. "Uh, ladies first, don't you think?"

"Isn't that archaic?"

"Do you read dictionaries for fun perchance?"

"Yes, why?"

"Never mind. As to whether it's archaic, it depends."

"Depends on what?"

"The woman and her mood."

"In other words, it's unknowable? Is that fair?"

"Fair . . . fair is an unapt, misapplied word used by people who are pertinacious. Any debate is over when *fair* enters the discussion. It's not a helpful word. And unknowable . . . oh, please, many things—maybe most things—are unknowable. If they weren't, humans would be bored as all get-out. Humans are terrible at knowing but great at coping."

Rusty nodded in agreement. "You want to go first?"

"No, you go ahead."

"But why did you—"

"I wanted to be asked."

Rusty opened his eyes wide and rubbed his forehead, remembering what his mother had told him about women.

"The tour bus is supposed to pick us up outside the hotel. You ready?" asked Odessa.

"Yep."

When the bus pulled up, Rusty and Odessa were the only people waiting to get on. Good thing, as the bus was almost full. They rambled to a couple of empty seats at the back. Only Turkish was being spoken. The bus had gone two blocks when it stopped to let a couple of people off and one person on. The same thing happened again in two blocks, and then again.

"What's going on with these stops?" Odessa asked Rusty.

"I don't know. I'll ask the bus driver."

When Rusty got to the driver, he said in Turkish, "Why do we keep stopping? I thought this was the tour bus for the castle."

"Yes, yes, it is. But this is also the island's public transportation. We will be at the castle soon."

Not knowing what *soon* might mean on Cornouss, Rusty asked, "You'll let me know when we're there?"

"Yes, yes."

About one minute later, four men stood up and pulled out machine guns from duffle bags. One of the men let out a short burst from the gun, and bullets pierced the roof. He said in Turkish, "Everyone be calm, and no one will get hurt. Driver, go on to the castle. And no more stops." Then he switched to English. "Abay, Ayaz, and Mirac, from now on we only use English to keep the hostages from knowing. Understand?"

The other three nodded.

Rusty and Odessa looked at each other, unnerved. When they arrived at the castle, all the passengers and the bus driver were herded into the castle foyer.

"Abay, go collect the wallets and such," said the leader.

After the wallets were collected, Ayaz began going through them.

The leader then told the bus driver in Turkish exactly where they were going, the route to take, and the bus they were planning to use.

Rusty heard every word.

Odessa whispered to Rusty, "What do they want? What are we going to do?"

"Don't know what they want. But we need to keep our eyes open for opportunities."

Ayaz, seemingly startled, rush over to the leader.

"Two of these be American."

"What? That cannot..."

Both had spoken loud enough for Rusty and Odessa to hear.

Ayaz shoved Rusty's and Odessa's passports at the leader. He looked at the passports and then at Rusty and Odessa. The leader and Ayaz whispered in English.

"Take them out," the leader said. "We cannot keep *them*. US Navy Seals are training on the west side of the island. We don't want to tangle about them."

Ayaz marched over to Rusty and Odessa. He had his gun pointed in their direction.

"Move," Ayaz said as he waved his machine gun hanging from his shoulder strap toward a staircase that went down into the bowels of the castle. Rusty reached over and gently took Odessa's hand, and they headed to the stairs. Just before they descended, the gunman said, "Stop." Ayaz stepped back a few feet and took out his phone. He typed with his left hand while keeping his right hand on the machine gun. His eyes darted back and forth between his phone and the captives. Then he holstered his phone. "Go," Ayaz commanded as he pointed the gun down the stairs.

They descended 101 steps and came to a door.

"Open," said Ayaz.

Behind the door was a dimly lit, long, wide corridor made of stone like the castle walls.

"Go," said Ayaz.

After they were about halfway down the corridor, Ayaz said, "Stop. Open the door."

The only door was on Rusty's right. He and Odessa walked over, grabbed the large circular metal ring, and pulled the heavy door open.

"In," Ayaz said. Rusty and Odessa walked into what appeared to be a large holding area with a high ceiling. Sunlight streamed in through barred windows on the far wall offering a spectacular view of the Aegean Sea. Ayaz closed the door behind them.

"For a minute there I thought we were goners," Odessa whispered. "You think they'll be back?"

"Maybe not. After all, they could have already killed us. Let's see if there's another way out. Just *look* at that view of the Aegean. It's to die for."

Odessa gave Rusty a shove, not at all pleased with the unbefitting humor. They went to the window anyway to see if they could fit through the bars. They could—if they wanted to fall one hundred feet onto rocks. Finding no way out, they sat down on one of the cold stone benches.

"Let's go check the door. Maybe we can block it so they can't get in," said Rusty. As they were fiddling with the door, they realized it was open. Well, not open per se, but it wasn't locked.

"Good gosh, did he forget to lock the door?" Odessa asked.

"Dunno. But let's push it open and scram."

While Ayaz was leading the Americans into the bowels of the castle, the other three were loading the other passengers onto the bus. The four terrorists drove away at the same time that Rusty and Odessa pushed open the holding area door. They quickly made their way out of the castle and down to the main road. They eventually flagged down a police car and explained what had happened. They were taken to police headquarters.

Once there, Rusty and Odessa were taken into the main room and told to sit. There was a flurry of activity with lots of chatter on the two-way radios. The police didn't care that the Americans were in the midst of the action as they were unaware that either of them spoke Turkish. Rusty could not hear everything.

The Turkish police captain said, "Omer, prepare the Pandora Team for insertion."

"But captain, we've never . . . I just—"

"In all our simulations, they have resolved terrorist situations with no deaths. Besides, the Turkish president's brother-in-law's father's maid's uncle is on the bus. I know the Pandora Team is the last resort, but we must use them."

"But if others find out about this Pandora Team . . . . And I myself have had doubts about the ethics of using—"

"Omer, you have your orders. Besides, we know the terrorists are wary of these two Americans. Maybe we can send them in with our Pandora Team. That would certainly distract the terrorists, which would give the team an even bigger advantage."

"Can you tell what's what?" Odessa asked Rusty.

"Some. The police have the bus surrounded on a mountain road, and they're trying to arrange an exchange with the terrorists."

"Exchange?"

"Yeah. It sounds as if they want to exchange the people on the bus for an abacus owned by Machiavelli and a bunch of Pandoras, whatever those are."

After slightly chuckling, Odessa said, "An abacus owned by Machiavelli? Your Turkish must be a bit rusty. Rusty—that's funny."

"Ha-ha." Rusty glanced at Odessa with his eyebrows raised and lips pulled to one side.

The police captain came over to speak with the two of them.

"Americans from the land of big salaries. Good thing you two check out. We need your help resolving this situation," the captain said.

"Our help?" said Rusty, looking skeptical.

"Yes. We're arranging a swap with the terrorists, the current hostages for some of our agents referred to as the Pandora team, and you two. If you'll do it."

"You're kidding," said Odessa.

"Not at all. The terrorists are a bit afraid of you two. That will help distract them from the activities of the Pandora Team, and we should be able to resolve the affair with no harm to anyone."

"If they are afraid of us, they might just go ahead and kill us. Besides, if they are afraid of us, they won't agree to include us in the exchange," Rusty said.

"Everyone we're exchanging, the Pandora Team and you two, will be dressed differently than usual. The terrorists won't know who we have included in the exchange until it's done. And because they are afraid of you two, they are less likely to harm you. At least not in public with US Navy Seals on the island. We have a change of clothes ready for both of you. Some of the people currently being held have medical conditions, so the terrorists aren't surprised we want an exchange."

"Excuse me, Captain, but you speak English quite well, better than most of the natives we have encountered," Odessa said.

"Boarding school in England, then Oxford," the captain replied. "Once you meet the Pandora Team, I'm sure you'll be easily persuaded to go with them. Follow me, please."

"Oh, so they'll torture us until we agree. Is that it?" Odessa said.

The captain laughed. "Nothing quite so dramatic. At least not in that way."

Odessa and Rusty followed the captain into a large room with only a table and a few chairs.

"Please have a seat. Omer is getting the Pandora Team," the captain said.

Odessa and Rusty sat down, both very puzzled and quite nervous. A minute later the door opened, and the ten members of the Pandora Team entered one by one, half of them male and half female. They lined up in front of Odessa and Rusty.

The first team member stepped forward and addressed them.

"Let me apologize that your trip to our island has been so, shall we say, eventful. But we implore you to help our Pandora Team bring this distasteful episode to a conclusion. I assure you we have experience with these terrorists and will do everything in our power to protect you."

The moment the Pandora Team entered the room, Odessa's and Rusty's mouths dropped open. The travelers were stunned.

"What in the Sam Hill?" said Rusty while looking at the captain. "You can't be serious."

"I assure you they have been well trained," said the captain. "Never has a hostage suffered even a hangnail when the Pandora Team was involved." That fact was true, after a fashion, considering the captain's definition of *involved* was unbound. "And they're going in, with or without you."

"Rusty," Odessa said, "we can't let them go in alone. If something went wrong and we hadn't helped . . . you know we could never forgive—"

"I know, I know," said Rusty shaking his head at the thought of helping, realizing neither of them could repel the request.

Rusty addressed the leader of the Pandora Team. "How old are you?"

"Twelve."

"And the other members of your team?" Odessa asked.

"We are all twelve, Miss."

"Why on the face of the earth would you let children do this?" Rusty asked, looking at the captain.

"You couldn't be in better hands, all things considered," the captain said.

Odessa and Rusty weren't as afraid as they should have been. Although their opinion of the authorities was low, the part of their brains tugging at *we can't let these kids handle it alone* was more powerful than the other part of their brains saying *don't do it . . . don't do it.* They were taken to a room to get changed and then escorted to the captain's office to go over the plan.

"There will be very little for you to do," said the captain. "Two things are essential. The first one is clear-cut. The Pandora Team will start playing a game once they're on the bus. It's called I Spy. Different team members will shout out the names of animals they see, for example, "cat." No matter what animal they shout, you are to ignore it. Ignore it completely. Do not react at all. This is critical. We'll practice this in a few minutes."

"How in the world will that help?" asked Rusty.

"After the first two or three animals are called out, the terrorists will get used to it, thinking the team is just playing their silly game. The terrorists will then become preoccupied with you two, allowing the Pandora Team to go to work resolving the situation."

"And what about us? What do we do?" Odessa asked.

"You are two smart Americans. I'm confident that you two can keep the terrorists at bay for three or four minutes. After all, we did find a copy of the book *Never Split the Difference* by Chris Voss in your room. A book about how to negotiate—even with terrorists. And three or four minutes is all the time the Pandora Team will need. Which leads us to the second thing you need to do: look for an opportunity where you can help."

At least there were only two things to remember.

As the hostages were walking from the bus to the police, the Pandora Team followed by Odessa and Rusty were passing them going in the opposite direction. After the exchange was completed, the *fun* began.

Abay gasped. "Look, look at who these are. Kids, they are—"

"I see. The captain has pulled a quicker one on us," the leader said in an angry voice. "But at the moment I am more concerned about these two. Ayaz, what are these two Americans doing here?"

"Dog," one of the Pandora members shouted.

The terrorist appeared startled for a second but quickly realized the kids were playing their silly game.

"What do you mean, 'What are the Americans doing here?' How do I know?" asked Ayaz.

"I told you to take them out," said the leader.

"I did. I took them out of the entryway," Ayaz responded.

"You fool, 'Take them out' means kill them," the leader said.

Odessa and Rusty looked at each other, eyebrows raised.

"Goat," two members of the Pandora Team shouted.

"What? No," Ayaz responded while pulling out his phone with his American English dictionary. "Look, see. No, it means to take away, to remove. I don't see . . . wait, that's at the bottom . . . that's slang. You can't expect me to know slang, you—"

"Sheep," several of the Pandora Team members shouted.

"You idiot," the leader said, wondering what kind of spot they were in.

"DUCK!" the Pandora Team screamed in unison.

Abay, who was sitting in the back of the bus, ducked his head so quickly that it hit the metal bar on the seat in front of him. He rolled into the aisle, out cold. Mirac, standing on the lower steps of the bus entrance, turned too quickly to duck and tumbled onto the asphalt, dazed. The leader and Ayaz, who were standing next to each other at the top of the bus steps, suddenly turned in opposite directions and got tangled up in each other's machine gun straps.

"Push," yelled Odessa.

She and Rusty shoved the entangled pair down the steps to join Mirac on the asphalt. By then the police were standing above the three—guns drawn.

The rest of Rusty and Odessa's stay on Cornouss was uneventful. When they arrived at the airport to leave, the captain was there to thank them again and wish them the best.

"I don't suppose there is a reward," Odessa asked rhetorically.

"The hospitality of the people during the rest of your stay. How about that?" the captain said.

"How long will the terrorists be in jail?" Rusty asked.

"They're due to be released tomorrow," the captain replied.

"Tomorrow?" Rusty exclaimed, both he and Odessa looking shocked.

"Yes, we told the Pandora Team if there were no injuries to them or you two, the terrorists would only be charged with disorderly conduct. Otherwise, they would be charged as terrorists and get thirty years. The Pandora Team was never in any danger—only you two. After all, the terrorists are the Pandora Team's parents."

The End

9

Braun, Victoria, and the Mob

Braun looked like the twin brother of Max Baer, Jr., when Max was on *The Beverly Hillbillies*: six feet four inches tall, 190 pounds, and the same face. I hadn't seen him for several days; to say I was edgy would be an understatement. He wouldn't have just vamoosed, not with our venture unfinished. The endeavor that he believed would land him Victoria, my sister, along with enough money to set us all up for life. I tried to ignore my anxiety that our plan—his really—had been discovered and that he had been chopped up into . . . . I stopped. Neurologists say you should avoid negative thoughts, as the negativity spreads throughout your brain and affects your overall state of well-being. The best way to be happy is to think you're happy because happiness spreads. After all, the easiest person to fool is yourself, which is why fake news has always existed and why I chuckle at pundits who believe that the truth will propagate because of the internet. Anyway, Braun finally did show up at my doorstep—with a police officer on each arm. But I'll get to that.

Braun was quirky. I wouldn't say he was paranoid, just extra careful. I couldn't blame him; after all, he used to work for the NSA. Braun didn't have a phone. He wouldn't even use a burner phone. He even convinced me to memorize ten words never to say on a phone because they would trigger a class-one review by the NSA.

I met Braun at my workplace, the bowling alley. He bowled a couple of games a week, always in the mornings. With the alley slow at that time of day, we got to talking until, before I knew it, we were pals. He was gregarious. For that reason and the fact that he was buff, I suppose, every other time he bowled a woman was with him. And it was never the same woman.

Braun would come to my house occasionally, which is how he met Vic—short for Victoria. Vic wrapped him around her little finger effortlessly and unintentionally. But then Vic could do that. She was attractive, had an IQ of 160, and by the age of ten was more socially adept than most adults. She had the face of Essie Davis, the brains of Mary Somerville, and the charm of Lauren Bacall if she wanted to be charming—or Marlene Dietrich if she wanted to be distant.

Braun had come over to my house. Actually it was my mother's house, but Vic and I lived there. Mom spent most of her time traveling the world. She had done that for as long as I could remember. *Mom* was the word for her station in life, but it wasn't a description of her activities. When we were younger, someone named Martha looked after us. As we got older, Martha moved out and only checked in on us occasionally. I called her my guardian, but Vic told me that *guardian* was just a hypernym.

When they met, Braun fell in love with Vic in seconds—or so he thought. And I use the word *love* loosely. The first time Braun saw Vic, we had walked into the kitchen, and she was at the breakfast table studying. She wore a sleeveless top, running shorts, and flip-flops, all of which were light blue. Vic's hair is black as coal and styled in a bob with her hair curling slightly in as it reaches her shoulders. Her eyes are a vibrant blue.

"Vic, this is my friend Braun. Braun, this is my sister Vic."

Vic glanced at Braun but didn't say a thing. She merely stood and headed over to get some more water.

"Vic, nice to meet . . . whoa, dude . . . you're quite the . . . I can tell we were destined to meet, me and a dang charming woman like yourself."

"Destined, no—fated, perhaps," Vic said as she returned to her seat and her calculus book.

"Destined, fated—who cares? How about I take you out tonight? We could do the town. I'm good friends with a couple of club owners. We could have quite a time."

"I have a Calculus II exam tomorrow."

"Calculus II? What college you at?"

"I'm in high school—a freshman. You'd better check the laws of this state before you take a girl."

Take a girl. I remember Vic telling me that *take* has more than one hundred definitions, including *to have sexual intercourse with*. I was pretty sure that Braun didn't know that, which was one reason why he was going nowhere with Vic—that, and not knowing the difference between destiny and fate.

"A freshman in high school? How old are you?"

"Jailbait," was all Vic said without looking up or changing her expression as she continued working on an equation.

"Did you know you can't starve in the desert?" Braun said to Vic.

Sighing, Vic continued writing and replied, "Yes, because there's so much sandwich to eat."

Braun burst out laughing. "So you've heard that one?"

I could tell Vic had had enough. She stood, waltzed over to Braun, and stared at him without an ounce of empathy.

"Speaking of sand, you need to shake the sand off your feet."

Braun looked down at each of his shoes.

"You're in quicksand and going down fast. Take heed. Before you know it, it'll be too late, miscreant."

Vic was driven to learn. She was averse to sex, drugs, and alcohol—"diversions," she called them. In time, perhaps, some of those diversions could be worth exploring. But for now, Vic found knowledge far more alluring, and she was unforgiving about certain things, including not knowing what words meant and how to use them correctly. And she hated the word *dude* with a passion.

"We'll pick another night then. I know some places under the radar. I guarantee you a good time. I've got references."

"Another night . . . I'm washing my hair. What a pity."

At that Braun and I headed out. Once we were outside, Braun asked, "What did Vic call me?"

"It doesn't matter. She just doesn't like you."

"Dennis, how many women have you seen me with?"

"Well—"

"That's right. And how many women have you been out with since we've known each other? That's right—zero. Vic's just being coy, playing hard to get. I've known women like that. And sure as eggs is eggs, she'll be mine."

I knew Braun was in love with Vic because of the project that Braun and I started a short time later. He kept trying to get her to love him, like an infatuated teenager. He may as well have been chasing the Cheshire cat. Infatuation is a phenomenon. You don't know the person, and the other person doesn't know you, yet you want them to love you. How does that make sense? People who are infatuated are immune to logic and reason even when they know it's infatuation. I knew another guy who had been infatuated with a woman and pursued her for a year. Finally, between boyfriends, the woman agreed to go out with him. But he couldn't stand her laugh. He found it vile. Infatuation seems ludicrous. What possible purpose can it serve? It's natural, people tell me. That's all people have to say sometimes—it's natural—which makes it unassailable. I read somewhere that love is never as strong as when it's unreasonable. I believe that now.

Our real problems started when Braun figured Vic would love him if he had money, lots of it. When he suggested the job, I said no because it was wrong—not to mention illegal. Illegal, technically yes, he admitted, but it would not be reported to the authorities. The first time Braun showed me his storefront and claimed it would set us up for life, I thought he was nuts. It was in an unfashionable part of town with a homeless shelter on one side and a community bank on the other. The entire block across the street was under construction.

"The construction racket will cover up the noise from our tunneling equipment as we dig to the loot."

"Tunneling equipment—I'm not about to tunnel into a bank."

"It's not the bank we're tunneling into. It's the homeless shelter."

"What the dickens! Why would we do that?"

"That's where the local mob keeps its money. It'll never report the theft. We'll give half of it away. Considering it would be ill-gotten gains and we'd be giving half of it to charity, we'd meet Aristotle's definition of ethical."

Wait, Why in the world would Braun be referencing Aristotle?

"You don't seem like an Aristotle kind of guy."

"I know lots of Aristotle's stuff because my mom is a Peripatetic."

What a coincidence, I thought, *so is my mother.*

"How do you know that the local mob keeps its money there?"

"Found out about it when I worked for the NSA."

"Okay, but if the NSA knows about the illicit money, the shelter would've been reported to the police and raided by now."

"Hah, small fry. Not even small fry. Teeny-tiny fry. At the NSA we'd spend more time listening to the bedroom recordings of world leaders, celebrities, and our relatives than we'd ever spend on a homeless shelter. It would never come close to being flagged. And if it ever was flagged, we could just unflag it."

We could just unflag it. What does that even mean?

"And Aristotle would believe it was, in fact, ethical—or at least not unethical," he said. For example, Braun explained, lying to the king would be ethical if the king were holding your parents hostage and would kill them if you didn't lie.

I thought perhaps taking the mob's money might, in fact, obtain Aristotle's imprimatur.

The fact that it was mob money explained why we were always disguised going into Braun's shop. It did get tiring disguising ourselves as women. And Braun was an awfully big woman. When I complained, Braun said success comes to those who go the extra mile.

We needed purses and women's accessories. Things didn't quite work out when I asked Vic to buy me those things.

"Vic, can you pick up a couple of things for me at the store?"

"Sure, what?"

"Makeup, lipstick, and such—a purse, a flowered wallet, and single-carry tampons. I need a quick lesson on makeup too. And about bras—what do those numbers and letters mean?"

Vic stepped over to me and looked hard into my eyes.

"Dennis, whatever you and your pal Braun are planning—stop." She walked off.

The FBI at the door wouldn't have scared me as much as Vic had. I was almost shaking. I knew I'd have to buy those things myself. And I stumbled when I tried. Of course I went to stores that I never frequented.

"Excuse me, miss."

"Yes?"

"Can you tell me where the portable tampons are?"

"Portable?"

"Yes."

"What exactly did your girlfriend say she needed? I'm assuming they're for your girlfriend and not your mother. I'm being generous with my assumption here."

I was taken aback. Was she making fun of me?

"Ah . . . she said she needed portable tampons. You know, the kind you can fit in your purse. Like this purse here," I said, holding up the purse I planned to buy.

"What size?"

"Size?"

"Yes, size."

"Regular . . . medium."

"Single use or reusable?"

Now I felt certain that the saleswoman was making fun of me.

"Maybe you can just tell me where they are, and I'll recognize the box."

"Aisle fifteen."

There wasn't an aisle fifteen, but I found them eventually. By then I didn't care about the size. I'd just cram one into my purse when I got home.

It was no cakewalk buying the other stuff I needed—panties, stockings, and a bra. Later I discovered I couldn't get the bra on. I couldn't fasten it, so I had to go back and buy a different kind—one that opened and closed in the front.

Dressing up like a woman was, pardon me, like hell. We'd get dressed up to go into the shop and undress once we were inside. Then dressed up again to leave. We spent more time dressing and undressing than we spent dressed as women. And I'm confident we didn't look much like women. If people got close to us, they would either stare or look away quickly. I told Braun it made us more noticeable, not less, but he ignored me.

And I had to avoid Vic, which was a nightmare in itself. Even though I avoided Vic when I was dressed up, she was too smart not to have sussed it out. I felt as if I were in a race with the mob, the law, and Vic. Then one day when I was partly dressed and about to click the bra closed, Vic walked into my room.

"I thought so," Vic said and then chuckled.

My mouth dropped open, and I dropped the bra.

"My guess is that Braun thinks I'd love him if he had money. And considering that you're overall an ethical person, I'd say you're planning to rob bad people."

I froze. At least I had on my black panties and my black stockings.

"Go on. Have a nice day. We can talk about this later. Oh, and Dennis, even if you're playing dress-up, I imagine briefs would still work." Vic turned and left.

Dang it, I hadn't thought of that. It took me twice as long to finish getting dressed with my hands shaking so. And my face looked a fright with my makeup job.

I met up with Braun a block from the store.

"Dude, you look uglier than usual. You look like—"

"I know, I know. Let's just get on with it."

While we were working in the tunnel, I was maladroit with everything I did.

"You're useless today. What's the problem?"

"Nothing, I just didn't sleep well last night." I lied.

Braun seemed to know exactly how to clandestinely dig a tunnel: what kind of tools to use, the power requirements, placement of outlets, how to dispose of the dirt, what kind of drill bits to use depending on the type of rock, and more.

"How do you know how to do all this?"

"The NSA. I was usually assigned to listen in on people digging tunnels, people like communists, bank robbers, survivalists, polygynists, witches, and polyandrists."

"Polyandrists?"

"One female supervisor seemed especially interested in them. But the witches were the most fascinating. Still, it made me wonder how many witches had to get hurt before they realized their spells weren't holding up the walls of the tunnel."

When I got home and was passing through the den, Vic said, "So, how's the digging going?"

I dropped my purse and stopped. I hadn't noticed her on the sofa. "Digging?"

"Dennis, I do the laundry."

Gee whiz, I didn't know if it was a blessing or a curse to have a discerning sister.

"Vic, do we have to discuss this now? The bra is killing me, and I think I got some makeup in my eye."

"The bra should be killing you; it's two sizes too small. And judging from this morning, your panties are too tight as well."

I stood there realizing I looked like a ninny. Part of me wanted to tell her everything. But I knew what she'd say: *Just stop*. So without another word, I went to my room and changed before heading downstairs at the sound of the doorbell. By the time I reached the door, Vic had already opened it.

"Yes?" she said.

I moved to the other side of Vic, stood slightly behind her, and looked out. My eyes widened, which was when Braun finally turned up. I thought about racing out the back door, but Vic always said that if you kept your cool, half the bad things that could happen wouldn't, so I didn't.

Braun was standing, supported by a police officer on each side. He looked groggy but coherent.

"Excuse us, miss, but this gentleman has been in jail for a couple of days, and the only thing he says is this address."

"We don't—"

"Jail!" I interrupted. "Why was he in jail?"

"He was in an elevator that got stuck between floors for six hours, and he had some kind of psychological reaction. He still hasn't snapped out of it. We assumed he lives here. We need the jail space."

"No sale," Vic said, and she slammed the door in their faces. She turned to me. "Your friend is a fool. He's wasting his razzmatazz."

"Vic, the police . . . you can't just—"

"Those weren't police; those were actors."

"What? How do you know that?"

"Dennis, there were plenty of signs. For one, their badges didn't match, and one of them was a sheriff's badge from Marion County."

"Marion County. Where is Marion County?"

"Not in this state. And they had toy guns in their holsters."

Vic never failed to amaze me. She had to be some kind of superhero. At least she was my sister, so I didn't have to be afraid of her—most of the time anyway.

I peeked out the window and saw Braun jerk his arms away from the two phony policemen as they walked away. Vic returned to the den, and I went to my room, falling into the bed and staring at the ceiling, wondering what to do. At first I questioned why Braun would try a stunt like that without telling me. But then I thought of several reasons he might.

I figured Braun would be back at his storefront the next morning, and he was.

"Gee," Braun said, "you look awful pretty today."

"Oh, shut up. That was a horrible trick you tried to pull yesterday. You should be ashamed of yourself."

"You of all people should know I've pulled out all the stops to get your sister."

"And how many times have I told you that's not going to happen?"

"And how many times does the impossible happen if a person keeps trying?"

I realized I was fighting a losing battle. Then I saw a man and a woman approaching us on the sidewalk. The man looked to be in his mid-fifties and was sporting sunglasses, a beard, a dark-blue suit, a white shirt, and a fedora. The woman was in her mid-thirties and was wearing a well-fitted bright pink dress and high heels. She looked like Siobhan Murphy.

Braun noticed the couple too, but he couldn't unlock the door fast enough to get inside before they were on us. After all, it can be difficult to find things in your purse quickly if you haven't had much practice.

"Excuse me, but do you have a light?" the man asked as he pulled his pipe out of his mouth.

"Sure," I said in a high-pitched female voice as Braun gave me an annoyed look. Normally I never carried matches, but they came in handy now and again when digging a tunnel. I handed the matches to the man, and he lit his pipe.

"Do you mind if I keep these? I left my lighter at home."

"Please do—"

"No, sorry," Braun said as he snatched the matches out of the man's hand.

The man didn't seem annoyed.

"My friend and I are from out of town. Could you show us where we are on this city map?" he asked as he pulled a map out of his interior suit pocket.

Because there was a slight breeze, I held one side of the map open while I pointed out where we were.

"Thank you," the woman said as she held out her hand to shake.

I shook her hand and said, "You're welcome."

The pair headed off, and Braun and I entered the store. Braun watched them from inside as they moved on.

"You nitwit," Braun said.

"What?"

"You have no idea who those people really are, and now you've given them your fingerprints."

At first I thought it was Braun's paranoia, but as we changed out of our women's clothes, I started to worry.

After we finished tunneling for the day and got dressed to leave, I saw Braun rubbing hundred-dollar bills on his face.

"What are you doing?" I asked with squinted eyes.

"I'll take you home and apologize to Vic for yesterday."

"But why are you rubbing money on your face?"

"People love the smell of money."

Braun was equating people with Vic, a major mistake, and I was thinking of Braun's face now teeming with more germs.

When we arrived at my house, Vic wasn't home. Braun was disappointed, but not for long.

"Look, Dennis, an envelope for me on the table. Is that Vic's handwriting?"

It was. Braun tore open the envelope. It looked like an invitation.

"Ha, Dennis! That's all I've got to say. And you said I didn't have a chance with Vic." He handed me the invitation.

It read as follows:

Braun,

You're invited to a gala I'm throwing at the Hilton this Saturday at eight p.m.

The invitation was embossed with the Hilton logo and had the specifics about the gala. "Invitation by Vic and Friends" was embossed across the bottom.

Braun was dancing in the foyer. "I'll see you later, buddy. Got to get a new outfit," he said as he ran out of the house.

I had an invitation too, just like Braun's. I started wondering, Would we need to finish the tunnel now? I didn't know what Vic was up to and knew I wouldn't be able to figure it out. Vic had told me earlier that she was spending the night at Suzie's. She would do that on occasion, or Suzie would stay at our place for the night. Suzie was smart too, and she and Vic often studied together.

My pleas to Vic went unanswered, my messages no doubt lingering as binary code on a computer chip inside her phone.

The next morning, the Saturday of the gala, as I was waiting for Braun outside his shop, a limo drove up. Two men in suits and ties stepped out and approached me.

"Mr. Vito would like a few words," one of the men said to me. The other man opened the back door of the limo and motioned with his head for me to get in while his jacket flapped open just enough for me to see the gun in his shoulder holster.

After entering the limo, I sat across from a man who resembled Michael Kitchen. He was dressed in a suit. The gentlemen who had offered me the invitation climbed into the front, and we started to drive.

"Dennis, that's quite an outfit you've got on. You do know you don't look like a woman, don't you? Well, maybe from far away, I suppose. Or to a blind man." He laughed. "Do you know who I am?"

"Mr. Vito, I suppose."

"Do you know why I want to talk to you?"

"No."

"Best not to say much. I understand. Braun's an interesting fellow, isn't he?"

"Braun?"

"So how's Vic doing?"

At that question, I lost my cool.

"Vic? Don't you dare—"

"Dennis, cool down, cool down. We're just talking. Vic's my daughter's best friend. I'm just asking."

"Daughter. Who's your—"

"Suzie."

Oh, God!

"Dennis, I'm just a friend of the family, after a fashion. Nothing to be concerned about. We're just having a conversation."

I never wanted to see Vic so badly in my life.

"Family is important." At that he pulled a picture out of his wallet and handed it to me. In the picture were Mr. Vito, Suzie, and it couldn't be . . . but there was Braun, and then . . . my God! I dropped the picture, and my mouth fell open.

"You can understand why I don't want Braun to get into trouble. And he will if your little project succeeds, serious trouble; deadly trouble shall we say. Some people in Chicago will be very unhappy, and I won't be able to intervene. I need you to handle things for me. What would happen if, oh, let's say you *accidentally* hit a water pipe and flooded your project?"

At that moment I didn't care a thing about Braun—or me. Why was my mother in that picture? Surely she couldn't have anything to do with this, this criminal. But then again, I didn't know my mother, not really. But still, it just couldn't be. It took me a minute to think of what to say. Even then, I spoke halfheartedly since I was completely drained.

"If I knew what you were talking about, which I don't, I would call it *Braun's* project, not *my* project. Besides, you have the resources to deal with Braun without my involvement."

"Yes, you would think so—but maybe I don't. Maybe he has something on me. You know, the NSA and all. That little cretin was supposed to be funneling us information like the rest of the cadre, but instead he decided to go rogue."

My gosh! On top of everything else, now I learned that the mob had infiltrated the NSA. I felt as if I had been hit by a tidal wave. I didn't know where to turn. I could barely breathe. It was as if I had been kicked in the gut. So where did all this leave me? I believed that Vic knowing everything would be the least of my worries.

Neither of us said another word.

After Mr. Vito dropped me back at Braun's shop, I went

home. Vic wasn't there, and she still wasn't answering her phone. I didn't know what was going to happen at the gala, but I knew I had to go. I had to talk to Vic. I just collapsed on my bed until it was time to get dressed. I put on my suit, tie, and Allen Edmonds.

As I walked through the lobby of the Hilton, I passed many a well-dressed couple. I grew more and more worried. Surely Vic, a high school freshman, hadn't arranged a real gala. I didn't see how she could, and even if she could, what would it accomplish? After mingling in the lobby for a bit without spotting Vic, I visited the front desk.

"Excuse me."

"Yes, sir?"

"Can you direct me to the gala?"

"You're referring to the annual police gala?"

"Police, no . . . ah . . . this gala." I fumbled while reaching into my suit pocket to get my invitation. "This one."

"Oh, yes, that's the annual police gala. Those invitations were printed for a few special guests, I'm told. Congratulations, I guess you're one of them."

Clang! I could hear the cell door closing behind me. But Vic wouldn't let that happen, Would she?

"Go down the hallway to your left, that way. Keep going until you see the sign and the ballroom. You can't miss it. Enjoy."

I found the ballroom, showed my invitation, and entered the room. There were a lot of people, but the room was so large that it didn't seem crowded. I was just hoping I could find Vic before I ran into Braun.

And then I saw Vic. She was wearing a long, flowing, sleeveless yellow dress with yellow high heels and looking lovely. That certainly wasn't the way to discourage Braun, but I had other worries at the moment. I hurried to Vic and started talking fast, really fast.

"Vic, I don't know what you're up to, but it's going to put me in jail. Braun and I have been tunneling into a homeless shelter to steal money from the mob. And Suzie's dad, Mr. Vito, he's a mobster. And Braun, I think Braun is his son. And Mr. Vito knows Mother. I saw a picture. Mr. Vito threatened me. He wants me to sabotage the tunnel, or I might end up in concrete shoes. I'm a criminal Vic, a criminal."

I turned to look behind me. I saw Mr. Vito, a henchman on each side, heading toward me.

"Vic, it's Mr. Vito. He's heading over to get me."

"Where?"

"Behind me. The guy who looks kinda like . . ."

But it was too late. Mr. Vito and the henchmen were next to me.

"Hello, Victoria," Mr. Vito said.

"Good evening." Then Vic looked at me. "Dennis, I believe you two have met but have not been formally introduced. Dennis, may I introduce Michael Kitchen. And Michael, this is my brother, Dennis."

"Michael Kitchen? No, this is . . . bloody hell." My mouth dropped open.

"Sorry for the charade, young man," said Mr. Kitchen, "but it was for a good cause. Your mother said to tell you hi, by the way."

"Mr. Kitchen was hosting an autograph signing in town earlier this week," Vic explained. "Susie and Braun are fans and had their picture taken with him. Mom knows him too and jumped into the picture. Michael's wife and Mom are both officers in the London Peripatetic Club."

At that moment, not far from us, I saw two police officers escorting Braun, who was handcuffed, toward the entrance.

"Oh, God, Vic. I'm going to jail."

"Dennis, Braun is an escapee from the Bodine Happy Go Lucky Asylum," Vic explained. "He stole twenty-five-thousand dollars from their fund-raising gala when he escaped. I've been helping the police capture him."

The End